TITAN
What awaited them in this frozen hell?

Jeffrey Peter Clarke

TITAN
What awaited them in this frozen hell?

DOUBLE DRAGON

Prologue

A brooding world adrift against the black infinity of space, Titan, largest satellite of gloriously ringed Saturn is like no other moon in the Solar System. A moon that would be a planet some have said; an analogue of Earth to those who favour analogues. Beneath a fog-hazed atmosphere of nitrogen suffused with layered hydrocarbon mists there lie continents. Continents with mountains, valleys, plains and vast dunes of organic grit. There are meandering streams and rivers, wind-rippled lakes and oceans touching the landforms with frigid kiss. There, too, in the perpetual twilight of this world, rain may fall and winds sweep across land and sea.

Like Earth? At minus one hundred and eighty degrees Celsius, water ice is granite-hard and forms much of the land. The clouds in the sky, the rain that falls to the seas below, they are not water but methane and highly complex hydrocarbons, some of which may in places freeze solid to form other landscape features.

What does this bizarre world, an alien place so far away, mean to the people of Earth, none of who had made the journey to witness first hand its forbidding realms? It is resources; resources of pressing desire to a sun-warmed planet hungering to replenish its own plundered assets. Titan reaches out. Titan beckons with a promise of largesse. Titan waits. But is this grim parody of Earth a world altogether devoid of life?

Jeffrey Peter Clarke

Chapter 1
The Man from Mars

If you are familiar with the events leading up to the declaration of independence on Mars then you'll recall how close to disaster came the human colonies out here. And even if you didn't, the whole affair cannot have passed unnoticed anywhere on Earth. Either way it will do no harm if I hover briefly over what happened since it has a bearing on the events that were to come.

What some people thought of as a kind of unblemished Eden was hardly the mythical garden of greenery but a very cold, many-cratered desert planet with a thin, unbreathable atmosphere. But for myself and others it was a retreat from the clamour and the distractions of an overpopulated, over-regulated and polluted Earth, a place where you could feel you mattered more, often far more, than you might on the home planet. As for those born on Mars, the majority by now of our population, very few opted for a permanent return to Earth as their goal in life because virtual reality could help make that all but unnecessary. Like anyone else living on Mars I can sit back, hook myself up, so to speak, and wander through all the sights on Earth. I can smell the gardens, tread grassy fields, feel sea spray on my face, know forest and mountain breezes, spend my spare time in any museum or art gallery with or without other people around me. I can explore any town and city as if I was actually there

7

and I can forget it's an altogether convincing illusion. Almost sounds like I really miss the home planet, doesn't it, but we do have our own comforts and diversions even if it's not possible to go out for a real time stroll to a neighbour's house.

None of the many permanent bases established on Mars could exist without its biodome. Each of these structures rests upon a great, circular basalt foundation, its bioplast shell grown organically over this solid base to form a vast, transparent enclosure, one large enough to accommodate gardens, modest woodlands and a wide variety of genetically programmed insects, birds and small mammals as well as our more discreet maintenance bots. All of these are devoted to the environmental upkeep of what are first and foremost the lungs of each base containing an atmosphere similar in composition and pressure to that of Earth, as well as places of recreation, somewhere for the kids to play and the nearest thing we have to Earth's outdoor cafés or restaurants. If you looked out to the desert from the perimeter path then you would see the true colours of Mars beneath a saffron sky but if you gazed upwards the bioplast shell had the sky looking as blue as you'd see it on Earth. A nice touch I always thought and most people would agree. Physiological adjustments have to be made for us all of course since on Mars we live in a gravity little more than one third that of Earth, but those adjustments are reversible should any of us return to the home planet.

Okay, so who am I and what am I doing out here? Well, I'm Commander Brett Anderson - just Brett to most people and no more than that for the purposes of this little tale. I was a pilot back on Earth but since most things that fly there have no need of a pilot I didn't have a great deal to do other than continue military duties that themselves were becoming obsolescent. My qualifications and experience in flying, however, got me out to Mars where pilots aren't essential either, but essential or no, they *are* wanted and they *are* in short supply. When cargo ships arrive from Earth, usually as containers entering Mars orbit rather than direct, their contents get distributed about the planet mainly in pallets carried by the kind of wingships it was my business fly. No other method for getting cargoes around is practical on our otherwise inhospitable world. For research teams, social gatherings and groups needing to move from one part of the planet to another, or to outstations where there is no runway, we have the smaller shuttlecraft. Like big insects, they can jump off, fly low altitude, go into orbit when necessary, and land just about anywhere.

Most of those travelling from base to base on wingship or even a shuttle want a real human presence up front, not an android or a virtual human allegedly in charge, but someone they could loosen up to with their complaints, their language and their away-from-base humour without what they say being overheard or recorded. Occasionally I'd take over the controls, just to prove to my passengers, or maybe more to myself, that I could be of some real use up there in our apricot sky. But other times I'd be flying alone with my thoughts and that I found truly satisfying because Mars was then my kingdom. At night, well used to the purr of turbines, I could consider my existence, dream my own dreams and admire stars undiminished by light pollution and shining in all their glory. In daylight hours I could make what I liked of those mountains, canyons and realms of cratered chaos, those immense volcanoes wingships had to skirt around because they were too high to fly over. Mighty Olympus in the northern hemisphere is over twenty-two kilometres from ground to summit and broad enough to cover the state of Arizona. And further south, on the Tharsis rise, a great bulge in the red planet's surface, a trio of volcanoes rise up to similar height, Ascraeus, Pavonis and Arsia. They stride across the planet north-east to south-west with Pavonis sitting dead on the equator. Then, dipping below the equator, a vast canyon system, the Mariner Valley, could reach from New York to Los Angeles and is wide enough to lose the Grand Canyon in one of its minor branches. All of this I find so fascinating that when I was approached some time back to quit flying and take instead a cosy position with the possibility of more elevated, official duties, I turned the offer down.

I was based at Novamerica One from the day of my arrival, one of the original permanent human habitations on Mars, though much expanded and modernised over the years – Martian years, that is, of six hundred and eighty seven days. Joe van Allen was, and still is, my base commander; in some ways a father figure yet also a good friend. He, too, belongs out here though he came initially on a five-year tour of duty. That was Earth years, by the way. The Martian year can make things a little complicated, though it has you sounding a lot younger for a while. Okay, so maybe from now on I'll stick to earth years. One of the longest established bases on the red planet, Novamerica One eventually became Joe's personal project and as base commander he saw it develop into what it is today. I'd not been on Mars very long when Joe, in considering what he thought best to serve my interests, and without me at first realising what he was about, manoeuvred me into the company of an undeniably desirable blue-eyed, blonde by the name of Karin. She was a planetary scientist, originally from Sweden and at the time was working for the Europeans at one of their own Mars bases. Despite my inner and sometimes verbal promises to others never to let it happen, I was soon hooked. We shortly after went through quite a lot together and I figure it's together we'll stay because that's what we both want.

As you may have guessed, bases with the prefix, 'Novamerica,' were once colonies of the United American States, just as other groups of bases once belonged to their respective power blocks back on Earth. That situation no longer exists but we never got around to changing the names. After the near total disaster I'm about to outline, the colonies decided to unite and go it alone. It had to happen some day and Joe, who'd been the colonies' chief negotiator during our troubles, was elected by all as president. Once independent there was no longer room for the kind of wasteful rivalry we sometimes had and we Earthlings were more than ever obliged to co-operate with one another. We had to be self-sufficient and trade with Earth, rare metals mainly, as well as research and manufacturing too difficult to carry out on Earth but not so in the wide-open spaces and lower gravity of Mars. We'd never do more than break even, though, because of shipping costs and the fact the powers that be on Earth no longer felt it necessary to go on supporting us to anything like the same extent.

As it turned out, Eden or no, and I'll just for now stick to old fashioned terms, there was a Devil who descended on us some four years back. His official function was to take charge of Frontier Mining and make it a more profitable concern for the shareholders and politicians back on the home planet. After bluffing his way over to Mars from Earth he almost brought annihilation down on us all. The guy in question, Virgil Hammond, had armed men, his own privately recruited little army, sent over in a space vessel driven by a totally revolutionary power source. Scientists back on Earth had tapped into so-called dark matter, that one-time mysterious gravity-related force that prevents the galaxies from flying apart. I was at the time told how the resulting propulsion system, which enabled the manipulation and reversal of that most fundamental of natural forces, gravity itself, would do to rocket power what steam once did to sail, only very much quicker. Yes, and we were soon to find how true that was, at least for dedicated space vehicles. The result was Aurora, and her like, a hyper-speed vessel that could cover in days what might take weeks by conventional means – rocket power, that is. Hammond intended no one in the colonies should stand in the way of his crazy plans – in particular, as it turned out, me.

But who helped us out in the end? Why, an entity we never dreamed existed or could exist; the incredible life forms that had thrived undetected deep beneath us, life forms that had the power to wipe the colonies off the face of our dusty little planet if they so wished. *Our* planet, we thought, but it was also theirs, the beings we referred to as Martians, though in their multiverse existence Mars was, to their seemingly infinite world, no more than a temporary stopover and we humans, initially at least, a curiosity, almost a source of entertainment. The Martians were a life form able to move through space and parallel realities and affect the present in a way quite incomprehensible to mere humans, though like we humans they were vulnerable to certain natural phenomena, including solar radiation and cosmic rays.

Initially, I said, until the bozo I just mentioned arrived with his private army to boost our mining operations and, using a part of the profits, set himself up as head of a new religious order on Mars. Extermination of the Martians went straight to the top of his list of things to do after his deep level drilling operations had gone through their kitchen ceiling and triggered a disastrous response that resulted in hundreds of deaths, by which I mean deaths of the colonists. If I have any claims to fame it could be my getting to know, as close as any mere human being could, the true nature of the Martians and for getting rid of Hammond personally, though I'll say no more about him for the time being. We newcomers from Earth now have at least one understanding with our cohabitants: we leave them in the voided regions they at present inhabit below the surface and they leave us to get on with what we think we ought to be getting on with upstairs.

***

I was down at base, strolling along the biodome perimeter pathway hand in hand with Karin, on the day this latest major turn in our lives began. She usually managed to take time off from her own work when I was at home base so we'd have a chance to relax together. We'd stopped for a while to gaze out across the morning landscape and the desert hills beyond when my left earlobe pinged. I reached to touch it and Joe's voice came through, 'Hi Brett, now you're on the ground for a while we need to talk. I see you're with Karin so how about you both come up here and join me for coffee.'

His message was casual enough but the tone of his voice and the fact that he'd tracked us down suggested he didn't want to be kept waiting. 'Okay, Joe,' I answered, 'we'll head up there now.'

14

'So he needs to see us both,' Karin remarked. 'Any idea why?'

'I have no idea at all,' I answered, 'but I'm sure we'll get a decent coffee.'

As we set off to retrace our steps a chime rang through the air. There would be another more abrupt chime some two minutes later. 'Sounds like they're going to turn on the rain,' I said, 'so coffee with Joe will save us getting wet.' There were occasions when we didn't mind getting soaked through and we'd hang about with that in mind when most other people headed for cover. We'd watch as the rain came down. It fell slower and in larger droplets than rain usually did on Earth because of our lesser gravity. Being established here on Mars where it hadn't rained outside for around three billion years may have had ourselves and others feel proud of the human achievements here over the last century or more but we still appreciated the odd rainy day. A number of bases still had ground sprays or hydroponics to keep their vegetation healthy rather than real rainfall from above and that made a few people jealous. I wondered about it sometimes – there must have been a last day on Mars when the rain fell, maybe no more than a gentle, diminishing shower. But still there must have been a last day. Anyhow, we took ourselves through the biodome airlock and up the stairs to Joe's office. Yes, the biodomes have their own main and subsidiary airlocks in case of those emergencies people hope will never happen; a stray meteorite, maybe.

In spite of his elevated position as the most prominent man on the planet Joe demanded nothing out of the ordinary in the way of home comforts and remained in the same modest office he'd always occupied. The door was ajar so we entered to find him stood gazing out across the runway beyond which stood the shuttle belonging to our base, and *Delta Seven*, the wingship I usually flew and thought of as my very own. There on show at the far side of Joe's desk was that cherished, ornate, nineteenth century mechanical clock he'd brought over from the home planet, always ticking away, never adjusted to the slightly longer Martian day and, so he claimed, showing the time at the mid-west town where he once lived on Earth. Joe smiled, stepped over to his never too tidy desk, gestured for us to sit and called across to the dispenser for three coffees. He always remembered, or at least the dispenser did, exactly how we liked ours.

'As I'm sure you know,' he began, 'The UAS and other interested parties collaborated with certain others on Earth to have a fully equipped commercial space station and laboratory that was designed to set itself up in orbit around Titan ready to take on a small crew.'

'Yes,' said Karin, 'some of my people were involved in its planning and construction in Earth orbit ten or more years back. The Titan space station, that's all it's officially referred to, is equipped for life support. It has a laboratory, as you say, as well as supplies to house up to six people for ten days, but human habitation was speculative

16

since at the time very few on Earth were convinced anyone would ever get out to it by rocket power.'

I knew something about the Titan space station also and I recalled it had taken almost seven years to arrive at Titan, but it wasn't clear to me right then who Joe was referring to when he mentioned 'certain others.'

'It's confirmed the thing had finished getting its act together at Titan less than a year back,' Joe continued as he slid our coffees across his desk. 'The first cargo vessel, just a glorified space tanker, arrives out there to join it in a couple of days time. The station itself is equipped with two shuttles that, when activated, are programmed to scoop up their load of methane as well as other trace compounds from one of Titan's lakes then deliver their cargos to the tanker vessel where it was to be sealed in for the journey home. But, once they have the tanker filled up with those hydrocarbon delights it will still take three and a half years at very best and maybe a great deal longer to get it back home.'

'That's what we were given to understand,' Karin said. 'But isn't it through the high cost of doing so why an increasing number of interests back on Earth are trying to get the whole project cancelled?'

'So a number of them are,' Joe replied, 'or should I say, were. Shipping methane back here was going to cost almost as much as the stuff was worth, if not more. But because of that the UAS, knowing they'd have an edge over everyone else with the development of Aurora, agreed to take over the entire show. With Aurora it became clear that Saturn and all of our Solar System would be accessible in a fraction of the time it has been and that included Titan. Those parties on Earth who dropped out reckoned they'd still be able to do a deal with the UAS once more processing facilities were operating around Titan because then there would be more than enough methane to go around.'

'So' I said, 'it's going to be a darn sight quicker and cheaper than sending out probes and robots on rocket power.'

'Exactly. I've been involved for some time in discussions with the International Council, with the UAS and with Frontier Mining so I can let you have an overall idea of what has been agreed as long as we here on Mars are prepared to go with it.'

'You mentioned Frontier Mining,' I said. 'How come?'

'The International Council and UAS,' said Joe, 'have agreed that Frontier Mining had to become involved.'

'You mean that outfit is still running loose around the politicians? I have to say I lost interest in them after they were kicked out of operations here on Mars.'

'Well they are still in business,' he replied, 'not big time on Earth but more so nowadays on the Moon. But the IC will be keeping a closer eye on them than before. Much closer, or so we hope.'

'And how is Frontier to be involved?' Karin asked.

'The UAS and other authorities on Earth had always regarded Titan and its resources as a kind of mining operation even though whatever they want from there will be sucked or dredged up rather than dug out. Frontier have offered to shoulder some of the costs as long as they have a worthwhile share in the profits. They did invest in the Titan space station years ago, before that lunatic, Hammond, arrived over here. Needless to say, they lost out big time financially through him and now they're itching to get some of their money back. Anyway, human beings need to go out there not to check on what we already know or think we know, but to look for what we don't know anything about at all, if you see what I mean.'

'I do see what you mean, Joe,' I said, and was about to ask another question when he continued, 'Back on Earth they're desperate for those resources and so are we now we have our own production facilities to support and further expand. Two days ago I concluded a formal deal with the UAS which means we, Mars, that is, are now fully involved. There's plenty of empty space here in our deserts so we're better situated to handle most if not all of the processing without any of the risks they imagine they might have on Earth. And access to such a wide and varied range of by-products will stimulate our home-based manufacturing. With more hyperdrive cargo vessels coming into service, Frontier Mining will be responsible for handling the incoming shipments from Titan. We'll process the contents here on Mars without their participation;

we'll place aside sufficient for ourselves then they'll send the major part, including a consignment of our own manufactured goods, on to Earth. We have the space and we have the technology even though our own needs are but a fraction of Earth's. As we'd expect, Frontier will have one of their own people out at Titan with the first crew so they can look at things in more detail and address any potential problems with the space station.'

Joe was right about the space on Mars, of course. The deserts on our sometimes dust-blown planet occupy about the same land area as on Earth but of course out here it's largely empty. And now was my chance to ask that question. 'You're telling us all this, Joe, as if Karin and I are somehow to be involved – am I right?'

He eyed our now empty cups and asked, 'Would you care for more coffee?'

We both said we didn't right then so Joe continued, 'Yes, you're right. But first, I expect you'll know something about DSV Orion.'

'Yes,' I replied, 'that's Deep Space Vehicle, Orion.'

'Yes,' added Karin, 'she's one of those new spacecraft developed from the Aurora we knew so well when she paid us a visit here on Mars - one that I'd rather forget.'

'Wouldn't we all,' Joe agreed, 'but Orion has been equipped for a first time mission to Titan and since Mars is supposed to be an equal working partner she's been allocated to us on a permanent basis as it's from here she'll be operating. I insisted upon this because processing the incoming raw materials would be our responsibility. It's a mission I want you, Brett, to take command of so I hope you'll agree, and I hope you, Karin, will be involved also.'

'Do tell us more, Joe,' smiled Karin.

'Well, Karin, you're a top-rated planetologist and I know you've made a special study of the Saturnian system. As well as that, no one would deny Brett here, with his experience and proven record of sorting out problems, one big one in particular I have to say, is by far the best man to take charge of Orion and the small team she'll be carrying.'

'But, Joe,' I said, 'this will surely be an historic event in space exploration as well as a business deal – the first human expedition beyond Mars orbit.'

'The first to the giant planets and way beyond Jupiter,' added Karin. 'We'll be making history.'

'So where is the lead-up?' I asked. 'Where's all the advance publicity? We've heard nothing until here and now yet we, everyone out here and Earthside should know all about this.'

'No it hasn't been up there in lights and there are a number of reasons why. To begin with, the UAS wanted to get to Titan before any competition on Earth and stake out their chosen area of operations. Then there's public interest to consider; everyone on Earth as well as here on Mars has been seeing what goes on throughout the Solar System since the twentieth century through the eyes of probes and robots. That has them thinking they've actually been out there and seen everything they'll ever want to see through virtual reality. And now with the likes of Orion and similar space vehicles under development, the journey times are no longer an issue and the risks are minimal on a ship fitted out with most of life's necessities. I guess it'll spark plenty of interest when you're on the way and much more so when you're actually there but until then we just get on with doing it.'

'Okay,' I said, 'I'll look forward to heading this operation.'

'And there's no way you'd be leaving me out,' added Karin. 'Why, this is – well, it's a chance in a lifetime.'

'But when,' I asked, 'will we be meeting this team and how long is the voyage out there likely to take – weeks, months?'

'Earth and Mars are not well placed at present,' Joe replied, 'but even so the team, or should I say the three of them, will be here in a few days as Orion's passengers. Orion will be in charge of them and not the other way around as she is designed to take care of her passengers. Okay, you asked about journey time. As we know, until now it used to take years to get out there under rocket power and even with Aurora we'd be looking at several weeks. With Saturn and Mars approaching their closest, however, we're looking instead at under four days with Orion's updated hyperdrive – Earth days so I'm told, for what that's worth. And an updated cargo vessel is to accompany Orion. The cargo vessel's own hyperdrive will be locked into that of the main ship until reaching Titan orbit and there Orion will release her.'

'Under four days!' I responded. 'But, Joe, that is incredible!'

Karin glanced wide-eyed at Joe then back to me as if asking whether I believed it or not.

'Yes, Brett, incredible,' said Joe. 'The stuff of dreams until quite recently. They learned a great deal from that first ship and her like and she's already on her way to becoming obsolete. Unlike Aurora, Orion isn't fitted out to take many people but will have on board a couple of four-seat helicopters or what people are referring to as skimmers. These are designed for descent to the surface of Titan where they'll be ideal for operations there. They'll fly over solid or liquid surfaces and set down on either and they'll have the ability to lift up certain objects of interest and objects of interest I'll get around to next.'

'I checked out one of those so-called skimmers, or something very similar, some while back in the simulator,' I said. 'They're easy enough to handle in Earth's atmosphere but wouldn't be any use here on Mars.'

'That may be,' said Joe, 'but in the heavy atmosphere of Titan, denser by far than that of Earth, a skimmer will be the perfect means of getting about. Now apart from collecting samples, there's a particular task for the skimmer you'll use if and when you have the opportunity and it should carry little or no risk. That task is to pick up the

Huygens lander that's been sitting down there since early in the twenty-first century.'

'Ah, yes,' said Karin, 'the Huygens lander was a very important event in space history. It was released by the Cassini spacecraft back in two thousand and five during her exploration of the Saturnian system and was the first human artefact to land upon Titan's surface.'

'And what are we intended to do with it?' I queried.

'Well, it goes into the isolation bay of Orion or into that of the new tanker vessel,' replied Joe, 'and will end up back on Earth where the Europeans plan to have it as a prize exhibit in their main space museum - it was one of theirs after all. There are plenty of other landers down on Titan now but this they want back home because, as Karin says, it was the very first human artefact to reach the surface.'

'And what about the older space tanker you mentioned as arriving soon at Titan?' I asked. 'As that's a rocket powered job sent out years ago I guess it will no longer be needed.'

'Oh, Frontier will have to decide whether or not to make use of it,' answered Joe. 'If so it'll do what's needed in its own good time. As for the new tanker, on reaching Titan orbit her automated systems will be released to co-ordinate with the space station shuttles. That's when and where your Frontier passenger will be able to take her over but he'll remain answerable to you as commanding officer. Sounds simple enough, I guess.'

'If you say so,' I muttered. The thought of our carrying a representative of Frontier Mining could never be high on my wish list.

'We've never resolved the question of life on Titan, have we, Joe,' said Karin. 'My own and other people have sent subsurface probes there but little we didn't know already ever came out of it so there were no great surprises except that – well, two or more of them sent back no information at all.'

'That's right,' said Joe, 'and that's another of the reasons why real people need to go there. Hopefully one of those probes can also be recovered though others are still transmitting. And there are, of course, a number of satellites, a few defunct together with a small number unregistered. We think three of these last may have been deployed by the TSS, the Titan space station, but I can find no information about their purpose and that leaves me feeling suspicious.'

'If some rival or undisclosed faction on Earth has plans to get involved,' I said, 'there could be danger could there not.'

Joe hesitated and looked hard at us both before replying, 'There's some rumour, or suggestion if you like, that a faction on Earth, one-time associates of Virgil Hammond in the UAS government, are out to gain *total* control of Titan's resources via Frontier as Hammond intended to do with ours on Mars. But that, nowadays wouldn't be so easy as they thought it was back then. Who might be backing them, how they could go about doing it and what, if any, danger there might be I have no idea though I've tried hard to find out. If it exists at all then there's a cover-up and that's why certain precautions are to be taken. One unknown factor in all this is the upcoming change in the UAS government presidency but I doubt their official interest in Titan's resources will be very different than they are at present, that is, get in first. Something else I'll tell you here and now, and this you keep to yourselves; after she arrives here on Mars, Orion is to be equipped with fully-integrated defence systems developed by ourselves, prepared and tested well in advance. We're able to do that kind of thing now but Earth must not be informed of it and nor must your passengers. I'm sorry not to have told you of all people sooner but I've been paranoid over secrecy until today.'

'Armed, Joe?' queried Karin. 'Why does Orion need to be armed? Surely that's not necessary.'

'Hopefully not but as the communities here on Mars were not so long ago vulnerable to the likes of Frontier and their influential backers it's important we have a sting in our tail. This is the first big secret we ever kept from the home planet and it has to remain that way for as long as possible.'

'You can take secrecy for granted with ourselves,' I said, 'and maybe I'll have that second coffee you offered us a few minutes ago. Something to celebrate, I think.'

'I'll have another coffee as well,' said Karin, 'and this will be my journey of a lifetime.'

Joe tried to suppress a sigh of relief as he said, 'Well I tell you now; if you'd turned this down I confess I'd have had sleepless nights in trying to figure out who else I might have approached. It may have ended up a completely automated operation or worse by far, entirely run by Frontier Mining with our own involvement jeopardised.'

'I'm sure we're flattered,' I remarked.

'We definitely are,' added Karin. 'And I think wherever humans can go, they should, otherwise what's the point in it all.'

Joe's old clock began to chime and it had me wondering for a moment where I was. He relaxed and said, 'Coffee? I have something stronger; a decent Martian bourbon, best taken straight. Better than the original back on Earth and we can drink to Titan.'

'You can count me in on that,' I said.

'And me,' grinned Karin.

'You'll both be able to familiarise yourselves with Orion and the space station at Titan the same way you do with almost anything else, through virtual reality.'

'And the set-up at Titan,' I asked, 'has anyone suggested giving the thing an official name? All I heard it referred to a few minutes back was the Titan space station or the TSS.'

'Er, yes,' mumbled Joe, producing a bottle and three glasses from his desk drawer. 'Some joker suggested calling it Miss Methany and posted images of it with that name plastered on the side as if *that* was official. It caught me the wrong frame of mind and had me thinking it made the whole operation sound like some kind of joke. I tell you if that guy was stationed here at Number One I'd have him transferred to our station at the south polar cap.'

'Then we'll refer to it only as what it is or the TSS,' I assured him, raising my glass.

'We really do promise,' grinned Karin.

But the Titan project, though not publicised as a high profile exercise would soon attract considerable interest here and on Earth. Orion, as Joe had indicated, would on arrival be stationed on Mars for a time, probably six days, during which she was to be fitted out and tested with our own equipment. Karin and I would have to familiarise ourselves with much of this. Before we left Joe's office I glanced out once more across the runway. Our shuttles would, at least for the foreseeable future, be powered by good old fashioned rockets as they could no way accommodate the fusion power core that concentrated and directed dark matter. As for *Delta Seven* and the other wingships, it seemed their time might one day soon be up. A pity since you get kind of attached to the ship you fly and we'd been through some tricky times together.

But returning to the subject of Titan; maybe you were thinking, why this grab for methane? There had been for a long time no demand on Earth for its use in generating electricity though it was needed for rocket fuel and would continue to be so where hyperdrive couldn't be employed as well as for many industrial purposes. I also discussed it with Karin who was pretty clear on the subject. 'Methane,' she informed me, 'is just a simple little molecule; one carbon surrounded by four hydrogen atoms but it's a precursor of nearly all organic compounds. Multiply the hydrogen or carbon or add other atoms or groups and you end up with many thousands of uses.'

Apparently we'd need nitrogen and oxygen as well to manufacture many of these fancy products. That would be no problem on Earth because it's what the air is largely made of but here on Mars we'd have to get nitrogen and oxygen out of ground sources or from our own thin atmosphere as we did for the biodomes.'

You may appreciate, then, why the surface assets of Titan were considered worth the effort once we had the means of doing it.

***

It was early morning at Novamerica One when, five days later, Orion entered Mars' navigational space. Karin and I had just finished breakfast in the biodome main café when Joe called us. In the days since that first meeting about the Titan project, Karin and I had a number of face to face discussions in his office, which he ensured was isolated from any potential eavesdroppers. We stood now looking out over the runway as DSV Orion appeared in the sky above, a silver, sleek and flattened form with no external features to break her lines. In defiance of gravity she descended slowly until around one metre above the ground where metal skis sprang out from below her to support the vessel once her motive power was cut back. Minutes passed before the ramp at her rear lowered and three figures in white space suits made their way down to the waiting ground vehicle. They would be welcomed into our reception area where their space suits would be stowed.

'Those are your passengers,' said Joe, who had previously briefed Karin and myself on their backgrounds and specialities. 'I have to get down there now, greet them and show them to their quarters. You'll be introduced to all three later this morning after which we'll take lunch together.'

***

Karin and I, when eventually summoned, left the biodome where we'd sat a while by the fountain to discuss the forthcoming journey. Wondering about the people we were about to meet we headed up to join Joe and the new arrivals in his office. After introductions we proceeded down to one of the smaller biodome cafés, set among trees some way from the main pathway and airlock where we could relax with birds singing and colourful insects fluttering by; all a part of our biodome ecosystem.

There was Viktor Saroyan, a slightly stout, round faced, dark haired man of around sixty. We were informed he'd had some involvement with the design team for the orbiting TSS and was a one time Frontier Mining executive but exactly how far up the scale he'd been Joe had been unable to ascertain. His aura of formal, self-importance was clear from the beginning. Sunita Chandra, a bio and organic chemistry specialist in her early thirties, was a slim, attractive, dark eyed woman with long, raven hair clipped tidily back. With her twinkling smile I expected she'd get on well with us all from the word go. Arnold Brendan was an attentive, sharp eyed, fair haired man in his mid-forties; a propulsion systems expert involved from the beginning in the development of hyperdrives used by the earlier Aurora and now by her successors. Nothing was mentioned about Orion's delay at our base so I figured Joe must earlier have given them a plausible reason for this.

At one point Karin said to Sunita Chandra, 'A visit to the Solar System's megastore of hydrocarbons must be of enormous interest to you.'

'Oh, but this is a dream come true,' she responded. 'I have studied most of the information sent back over so many years by probes and satellites but actually getting close to Titan, you know, actually *being* there at the real thing, will be something else.'

'Quite,' I agreed, 'there's nothing like sending humans even though virtual reality is so – well, so virtual. And there's a small hotel waiting for us out there when we arrive. What more could we want.'

'I appreciate your enthusiasm,' said Viktor Saroyan, alerted by my reference to the TSS, 'and I imagine the accommodation on board the Titan space station, for which I am at least partly responsible, would prove satisfactory if in the unlikely event you should have need of it, that is.'

'Would there be decent room service out there if we did?' I asked him. Karin grinned, as did Joe, Sunita and Arnold. They glanced at Viktor for a response but he appeared puzzled at my frivolous remark and I began to wonder if he'd taken me seriously for he made no comment.

'Maybe there *will* be someone waiting out there to greet you all,' quipped Joe. 'Or some thing.'

'Oh, I do hope not,' smiled Sunita. 'What could possibly live in a place like that.'

'It's rather odd, though, don't you think,' said Arnold, 'that in spite of all that's been sent out there I believe we still have much to find out concerning Titan's interior.'

'We know it's rather complex and it's certainly been difficult to study,' said Karin, 'but perhaps we'll learn more when we're down there. Pity, though, we won't even be able to touch the ground with our feet in most places.'

'Oh, why is that?' queried Arnold.

'Because, even wearing our environmental suits,' she replied, 'the modest heat of our bodies getting through would cause the ground to melt where we stood and we'd probably sink right through.'

'Talk about digging your own grave,' Arnold responded. 'Titan doesn't sound like much fun to me.'

'Titan is not meant to be fun,' said Sunita, raising a finger, 'but it will be very, very interesting, I know it will, and I'm sure there will be surprises.'

Viktor Saroyan maintained an indifferent silence, relaxing in his seat and eyeing Sunita Chandra several times until our food, humming along on an automated dispenser arrived at the table. We continued on with small talk until after lunch when Joe offered to show our guests around the biodome, then parts of the base, including our laboratories and food processing plant, this last being one of the facilities we expected could in time benefit further from the abundance of organic raw ingredients Titan had to offer. Karin and I remained at the café a while longer after Joe escorted our new arrivals from the biodome. With time to spare we set off for an afternoon stroll about the perimeter path until Joe called for us once more.

He was alone when we entered his office and had me close the door, which he often as not had left open. 'There's something I didn't mention earlier for obvious reasons,' he began once we'd had the inevitable coffee dispensed. 'I had those three scanned by our security system on arrival as they passed through the main airlock; the one we had installed a few years back to ascertain that anyone entering the base was really as human as they appeared to be. I doubt our visitors would know anything about that since it was never communicated to the folks on Earth.'

'And?' I asked.

'Well they check out genuine humans and all appear to have undergone standard physiological compensation to deal with prolonged Mars gravity both here and its equivalent onboard Orion. That guy Saroyan, however, does have a number of artificial bits and pieces including his heart – nothing unusual there except for one other implant embedded in his upper sternum. It resisted our attempts to resolve exactly what it's doing there or what it's purpose is. Stranger still, our technical team think it may have informed him of our efforts and that I do *not* like.'

'Can you not question him over it?' I asked.

'Sure, I could but if he didn't want me to know its real purpose then he'd probably grab some off the shelf reason to keep me happy. No, I'd rather make nothing of it now and give him sufficient time to maybe reveal its purpose. Could be it's not important but I'd still like to know and I think you should also.'

***

The six days during which Orion was grounded, modified and reprogrammed for our own use on our forthcoming journey followed without incident. During this time Karin was called away to other duties and departed aboard one of the European shuttles. Joe arranged for me to take our intended crew out for the first of two scenic day trips in our ground vehicle and get to know them a little better. This would include a visit to one of our research stations some twenty-five kilometres west of Novamerica One. We entered the pressurised, bay wearing our crew suits and on seeing our wide-tracked, blue and white ground vehicle Sunita exclaimed, 'Oh, she looks like a huge beetle!'

The two guys in there for maintenance duties grinned and appraised Sunita with undisguised admiration before quitting their task and I have to say I couldn't blame them. Once through the small airlock - this only accepted four people at a time – or two had we been wearing pressure suits and back-packs - we passed along the centre of the GV. Here were lockers, bunks, wash cabin and the small laboratory; each a triumph of ergonomics and engineering. The ground vehicle was designed to accommodate four people for up to two weeks. The control cabin was meant for only two but those seated further back could easily see out to admire the scenery. The GV was not pre-programmed for our modest excursion and even had it been, I still intended to drive. Our display showed the decrease in pressure inside the bay. As it dipped below ten millibars, on its approach to Martian air pressure of around six point five, first the inner then the outer airlock door slid silently upward. The temperature reading for outside hovered around minus eighty-five Celsius.

Conversation during this first excursion across the desert touched inevitably upon the subject of our planet's other residents, the enigmatic Martians. Arnold was curious to know all about them in an almost disbelieving kind of way whereas Sunita was unreservedly fascinated. Viktor remained silent for a time. As the cratered landscape drifted by, Arnold and Sunita asked me to describe them, she pressing hard to know more. Answering their main question was something I was not able to do other than to point out that, 'They looked like whatever they wanted me or other people to see.'

'I take it they are no longer a danger,' remarked Viktor, who now showed some interest in the subject of our conversation.

'A danger!' I responded. 'They never set out to be anything of the kind. They were only a danger when Frontier Mining began using plasma drills and their onetime boss planned to wipe them out. Nowadays it's a matter of live and let live and you'd no longer know they were on the same planet as ourselves. You know, I sometimes wonder if they still are.'

Viktor shrugged and made no more than superficial comments. I was convinced by now that he resented the involvement in the Titan project of another party, namely Mars, even though it had all been agreed under the jurisdiction of the International Council for what seemed, even to the UAS, like sound economic reasons. The visit to our outstation, where mineralogical research was being undertaken, broke the journey and the day ended when we returned to base in time for dinner.

Viktor did not join us for the second trip out in our ground vehicle but the following day Joe informed me Orion was cleared to speed us on our journey – one that you recall was to take less than four days; an idea that still, for me at least, had some getting used to. Then, I thought, with Mars and Saturn in their present positions it would take light itself only around seventy minutes. That helped to recalibrate my sense of perspective a little.

In the days before we were to leave Mars I had undertaken a real time, actual presence pre-voyage assessment of Orion. On what was anachronistically referred to as the 'control deck' and in earlier times the 'bridge,' there were no controls at all. There was instead seating for six people to relax, if relaxing was possible, and take in images and information generated at the big display area directly before us in what was the bow of the ship. I could establish control of Orion by voice alone if necessary, provided she considered me sane, but that would be pointless, detrimental perhaps until we reached our destination, and even then why might I need to do that? The size of Orion allowed for comfortable crew accommodation as well as private facilities, and there was, of course, programmed dreaming and extended sleep we could take advantage of to ease the journey. I wondered what fantasies the three from Earth might let themselves into on the way out.

My thoughts turned to the Titan space station waiting for us in orbit around that distant fuzzy moon, itself in orbit around Saturn once every fifteen plus days. We would lift off the following morning at around ten o'clock local time to set out on our long journey to this still charismatic moon.

Chapter 2
The Voyage of Orion

We suited up that morning in the main concourse with Joe and a couple of his colleagues standing by as we exchanged small talk. Viktor chatted briefly to Joe and to Arnold but with no one else. Karin and I as well as our co-travellers needed little help in pulling on the environmental suits because, though well insulated against cold and radiation, they were lightweight. They'd keep you happy in the vacuum of empty space for a while but if we were going down to Titan's surface they were designed to protect us, should we be exposed by mischance, to a totally unbreathable and deeply frigid atmosphere at around sixty percent higher surface pressure than that of Earth. We needed the suits now for the short stroll to Orion as no one so far had figured out a more convenient way of getting to and from the various kinds of ships that landed at this or any other base. Had this been Earth, I wondered if we might have had a grand scale official send-off, though it wouldn't have suited me in the least.

'Are you going to wish us luck, Joe?' Karin asked.

'I sure am,' he replied, 'but I hope luck isn't needed anywhere along the line.'

'I guess Orion will keep you informed of everything, Joe,' I added, 'even the speed our fingernails are growing.'

'Fingernails!' laughed Sunita as she lowered and fixed on her helmet. 'Oh, surely not!'

Orion would, throughout the journey, be monitoring the health and condition of us all though I wasn't sure I wanted that too much – at least not for myself. I determined to cut me, but only me, out of her scrutiny except for anything pretty damned serious. Anyhow, Joe stepped over with us to the inner airlock doors and raised a reassuring hand as they closed. We waited as the airlock depressurised and the outer doors slid open to allow sunlight and red Martian sand to finger its way inside. No one spoke as we strolled over with our cases to ascend the boarding ramp at the rear of the vessel. Standing aside to let the others by, I turned to look at our administrative buildings and other structures, then to gaze up at the vast form of our biodome curving away into a saffron sky. Okay, I lived there, but as always I felt pride in what humanity had achieved over the decades on the cold and dusty little planet I and so many others now called home. We were very soon to head for somewhere more distant; to a world more strange, more hostile by far, yet one that beckoned us from across the vastness of space.

With the boarding ramp raised and the airlock pressurised, the inner doors slid quietly open and we stepped into the main body of the vessel. Inside the suit storage and sterilisation area we loosened and lifted off our helmets and Orion announced, in a reassuring but well articulated female voice, 'Welcome aboard everyone. Once you have stowed away your environmental suits, please proceed ahead to the control deck in readiness for departure.' Her next communication came to me through my earlobe, 'Hi, Brett, I'll await your instructions. Though pre-programmed I may of course be redirected by yourself at any time or, should you be indisposed, through your second in command, officer Karin Blomdahl.'

'Thanks for that,' I muttered. Yeah, we'd decided during her stay at base that Orion and I would be good pals on first name terms, and should I end up wacko then Karin would take over my job. In spite of the name, Orion, our spacecraft would be, as ancient tradition continued to insist, a 'she.' I was aware from the knowing smile on her face that Karin had been copied in on the message. I'd had a personal friendship with my wingship when flying cargoes so why not here since I was supposed to be in charge. But as mentioned I doubted I would have cause to interfere with the vessel we'd all be relying on.

Once in their day to day crew suits the two women had let down their hair, Karin's corn blond to contrast with Sunita's shining black. I noticed Viktor eyeing Sunita as he had back at the base but then, why not; like Karin she was a woman to catch the attention of most men.

We stepped along between the accommodation, storage units and gymnasium, then there was the power core, with which Arnold would have by far the greatest familiarity. Next we passed close to the bay containing the two surface skimmers intended to allow us a more intimate look at Titan once Orion was in orbit there. As you'll have gathered already, DSV Orion was a good sized vessel. Further along at the control deck we took five of the six seats, where there were arm rests but no seat belts. We relaxed in comfort to observe the main forward display where Orion could materialise images at will, or we could peer through virtual windows at whatever was going on outside. There a number of pressure-suited maintenance people had stopped what they were doing to watch us depart when I murmured, 'Okay Orion, let's be on our first stage.' Lifting off would be a strange experience for anyone used to rockets or even wingships because there was naturally the noise associated with them and you'd be pushed back hard or very hard into your seat. A triple chime rang out followed by no more than a gentle humming and we all knew what it meant. The words, 'Departure initiated,' materialised before us but some moments passed before I realised we were moving – not just moving but accelerating though we felt not a hint of g-force. The base was receding, we were looking down on the biodome, a precious but diminishing bubble of life in the red desert. Then at the wider landscape. Our visitors from Earth had already experienced this mode of transport, of course, and Karin and I had plenty of virtual reality experience, but this was weirder because we *knew* it was real. The sky was rapidly darkening and soon, behind and to our left, appeared the immense, sprawling bulk of Mount Olympus and her cratered summit. The sky about us was black and, approaching the equator, we saw passing below us the Pavonis volcano and its two close companions; Ascraeus in the northern hemisphere and Arsia in the south. I had thought of having Orion announce and describe these truly impressive features but maybe that wouldn't have suited everyone and Karin knew pretty well everything there was to know about these amazing features anyway. My own knowledge was gained mainly from flying experience – trying to get around them, that is. We'd soon risen high enough to match orbit with the Isaac Newton space station and could see her ahead of us, glinting raw sunlight on Orion's main display.

To those not familiar with our space station, it's by far the largest artificial object in orbit around Mars or any other world except for Earth. A great, double-walled cylinder, it began as a wheel and was added to over many decades by new prefabricated sections sent out from Earth. All life there exists between those double walls so that if you're aboard the station, the inner wall is your ceiling and the outer wall your floor. The whole thing rotates to simulate Mars gravity but through the profusion of virtual windows you would see Mars below or the sun and the stars beyond as if you were not rotating at all but in regular orbit. You'd get used to life there as long as you didn't try to hurry anywhere at an angle out of line with that of the rotation. The power core is close to the hollow centre and at the far end is the detached, fully automated observatory. Nothing larger than a shuttle could dock with the station and that involved a tricky manoeuvre. On arriving, a vessel would enter the cylinder, turn its tail to face the inner wall, match the rotational speed then descend to one of the airlocks. Attempting to do that manually would spoil my day but then I don't recall anyone had ever set out to try it. The station used to belong entirely to the International Council back on Earth and in its earlier days carried emergency supplies for the colonies. Emergency supplies are no longer needed and ownership of the station is now shared between the IC and Mars. I called up Amalia Barbosa, one time Administrator for Colonial Affairs. She had in those days worked hard for the colonies, supported our bid for independence and later opted to retain her position as station commander. She was also our ambassador to Earth and joined Joe, myself and others every so often down at base. Joe had copied Amalia in on our project so her image appeared before us, smiling large, to chat briefly with myself and the others and to offer us bon voyage.

Shortly after we'd be passing above Mars' evening terminator and crossing the dark side of the planet where a scattering of lights far below confirmed human presence, but the space tanker was already in view. Orion closed in and we drew alongside some ten metres away. The vessel was fatter and slightly shorter than Orion, and though possessing her own power core and hyperdrive unit she would be locked into our own navigational system until being released at Titan to enter programmed co-ordination with the TSS. It was here that Viktor Saroyan would become more fully involved. Involved in ways I could never have imagined.

'We are fully integrated with the cargo vessel and await your go-ahead,' came Orion's voice. On the main display glowed, 'Departure procedure optimised.'

Despite the immensity of the voyage ahead, this was beginning to feel, almost, like some kind of scheduled flight. I glanced at my passengers. Karin smiled back at me, Sunita and Arnold were looking straight ahead in expectation but Viktor was staring down as though absorbed in his own realm of thoughts.

'Let's go, Orion,' I breathed. The main display showed, 'Main departure sequence initiated,' and a single, prolonged chime sounded all about.

Karin and I, instinctively expecting more physical feedback from this stage than on our ascent from Mars, sat in tense anticipation and, eyes closed. Moments passed then she asked, 'Is anything actually happening?'

It certainly was. I looked to my left at the virtual window to see Mars slipping away behind us, slowly at first, with the distant sun swinging into view and I answered, 'Yes, it seems we're on our way.'

With our speed and acceleration showing on the main display, and both climbing at a truly astonishing rate, I still marvelled at the fact we were not crushed back into our seats far more than we ever could have been within a rocket shuttle or even a wingship – hard enough to render all five of us flat as pizzas. But no, as Karin and I had been assured by the simulations and then by Arnold, that the forces propelling this vessel, large as she was, acted equally upon everything within it, like something gripped every bone, every nerve, every molecule in our bodies. Our three guests had experienced it on their way out from Earth but to me, as it must have been to Karin, this was indeed a strange though far from unpleasant sensation. It seemed we'd eventually be travelling away from Mars and from the sun at around sixteen million kilometres per hour with the cargo vessel and ourselves locked within a common force field.

'This is amazing,' said Karin, 'we might almost be standing still.'

'We're moving a lot faster than when we headed out from Earth to Mars,' confirmed Arnold, 'but then there's so much space junk floating around back there we needed to take more care. My team and I are working even now upon Orion's successor. It will transport us to the very limits of the Solar System and far beyond.'

'To the stars one day, do you think?' queried Sunita.

'That doesn't seem to be an option if you believe old Einstein,' I replied. 'But who can say.'

'But who can say,' repeated Viktor from the seat behind me. 'I thought by all accounts those creatures of yours on Mars could move anywhere through wormholes in space-time. You could have asked them how they did it since you got to know them so well.'

'Let me tell you,' I replied, turning to face him, 'first of all they're not *mine* and nor are they anyone else's. They're not creatures either but a highly intelligent life form who want nothing more to do with us, and I can't say I blame them after what happened back there.' I'd earlier begun to realise I wasn't going to get on as easily as I ought to with this guy, though I told myself I had to make the effort.

'But now at least we have Orion,' commented Sunita as rapidly increasing performance information continued to impress us as nothing else could, 'and we can go a long, long way.'

'So we can,' Arnold responded, 'although there are theoretical limits to her performance the system powering this vessel will presently allow. But then it was once said man would never go to the Moon or to Mars.'

'And now,' said Karin, 'we're entering another new age of human exploration. For me this is a most wonderful experience.'

'Anyone for Pluto?' I asked.

'Well I wouldn't mind if I'd packed a few more things,' she grinned.

'Oh, but I do not think Pluto would be as interesting a world to explore as Titan,' declared Sunita.

'Pluto has a sub-surface ocean like so many other bodies in our system,' added Karin, 'but there's little or no atmosphere or surface activity to speak of.'

For a while no one spoke. We just peered up at the main display or at the virtual windows and saw now only bright stars. Odd; at the speed we were going I half expected to see the stars moving. 'They don't look much different than they do from Mars,' I remarked at last.

'No, of course they don't,' said Karin with an amused, 'Tut-tut' expression on her face.

'I think it a pity we will not see Jupiter and her moons,' remarked Sunita. 'What a sight that would be.'

'No,' said Karin, 'Jupiter at present is half way around the other side of the sun – but as you say, it's a pity about that. Perhaps with Orion we'll get to explore there another time. For now, I'm happy with the stars.'

Maybe, so I thought, we would explore Jupiter another time but our attention was drawn further to the big display before us that appeared to have dissolved away the entire front of the vessel so we now looked straight out into space. It seemed Orion, noting our interest, or perhaps with a discreet request from Karin, had decided to enhance our experience. Even I found that a little unnerving at first but Karin and Sunita were captivated. Arnold stared open-mouthed and Viktor sat with his head once more lowered except for an occasional upward glimpse.

The stars in their glory seemed to beckon, certainly to draw me ever on into boundless realms. The void we had entered was immensely further away from the sun than anyone had so far been and that in itself imposed a kind of reverence. As I gazed out mesmerised, lost to infinity and hardly aware of those sitting close by, there was a brief flash to one side. We'd sped past something relatively close, though it had to be thousands of kilometres away – a wandering asteroid, maybe. This was confirmed a second or so later by Orion but it had shaken me back to the here and now. 'Look,' I said, 'let's explore something else, the food facilities I mean, and have ourselves something to eat.' I felt almost guilty over breaking the silence then Arnold agreed, 'A good idea, Brett, yes.'

In the area allocated for food dispensing and eating, a triumph of ergonomics like our ground vehicle, there was room for six people, had there been a full complement, to enjoy their meals in reasonable comfort. The menu offered by the molecular processor, an example of how flavours and textures had improved over the years, could convince you that you were eating or drinking almost anything within reason. Out of sheer necessity the greatest improvements in that respect had been made on Mars through our own developing industries. Conversation, while we ate, centred upon Orion, upon Earth matters then back to Titan. Arnold explained as much as was understandable to us about dark matter, gravity and the very propulsion system that now was hurling us at phenomenal speed toward our goal. In his enthusiasm he made it sound as if he'd developed the system mainly by himself. This was not altogether true, of course, but the guy had to be clever and was quite entitled to boast. Here Viktor showed considerable interest since it was the hyperdrive that had rendered Frontier's planned operations at Titan feasible.

We returned to our seats on the control deck, had a verbal and graphic update on our position from Orion then resumed small talk. Engaging least of all with any of us, Viktor seemed ever taken with his own thoughts and I noticed him, as I had earlier, narrow-eyeing Sunita for brief moments. Eventually the subject of sleep was raised by her and with the work and pre-ordained rest periods in mind, we agreed this was not a bad idea. Karin and I took the quarters prepared for us; compact, yes, but with all the features we could reasonably need. Very thoughtful of Orion's designers was the facility for pre-selected and shared dreaming.

'D'you think the others will be choosing dreams of their own?' I asked Karin as we prepared ourselves for bed.

'It wouldn't surprise me if Arnold dreams about his next hyperdrive project,' she answered.

'Could be he will – Earth to Neptune and back for a long weekend trip.'

'And Sunita; there can be little else on her mind other than Titan, or can there?'

'Doubt it,' I answered. 'As for Viktor, I reckon he might try to dream about Sunita though it's that implant of his that bothers me.'

'So you've noticed him eyeing her, have you?'

'A couple or more times, yes,' I replied, 'but there's probably nothing to it other than a passing fancy. Maybe it's the first tank-full of methane that'll fuel his night-time fantasies.'

'Yes Brett, dear, what else,' Karin laughed. 'Methane fuelling his night-time fantasies - the very thought of it! I hope you'll come up with something better.'

'You can bet on it,' I breathed as we pressed closer, 'and we know what it is don't we -- yet another first this far from the sun.'

Next would come sleep. Then our dreaming.

We were back together in the biodome at my home base on Mars, stopping on the perimeter path to gaze out over the Martian desert and at the slender clouds of carbon dioxide ice hanging as iridescent streamers that glowed in the sun at around fifty kilometres high. We left the path to stroll along a lane through a wooded area, listening to chirping birds and humming insects, catching sight of furtive little mammals, all genetically modified, all programmed to play their part in our artificial lives. We emerged to sit by the central fountain and there we stayed, just listening to the magical play of water on that driest of worlds.

***

It was morning. At least that's what the light showing around the edges of the virtual window tried to convince us it was. Karin looked at me and sighed, 'You know, I woke up thinking we were back on Mars. I wonder if I'm still dreaming even now.'

'Maybe the whole of life is a dream,' I said peering at the virtual window. I had the false dawn effect cancelled as we both felt it not in the least convincing since there is no morning or evening in deep space. Once showered and wearing our crew suits we joined the others for an unhurried breakfast, prepared in advance by Orion. There much verbal speculation ensued, even from Viktor, then we gathered on the control deck to view graphics of our trajectory and other details pertaining to our journey. Apart from the control deck and our quarters there were few places to go other than the ship's laboratory and small gymnasium. I decided to drag myself along to the gym later and hoped Karin would join me. First, though, I decided to do what I ought to have done before we left Mars; clue myself up a little more on the characteristics of Titan. Meanwhile, Orion, knowing full well the physical dispositions of her crew, though only the basics of mine, had asked us if all was as we wished. She not long after that informed us we'd passed through the Asteroid Belt and later during that daytime period we would cross the orbit of Jupiter – something of a non-event since we knew the greatest of all planets wouldn't be there. I peered at the nearest virtual window to find the stars looking much the same as they had the day before. Visible close by on the other side was our one-way companion, the space tanker.

Later on, after we'd viewed another situation update, Arnold suggested we watch some ancient twentieth century movie; one about a lethal alien getting aboard someone's spaceship. Sunita agreed, as did Karin and I but Viktor excused himself saying he needed to discuss financial matters with his associates back on Earth. I didn't bother to ask Orion how many light minutes we were away from Earth at the time but I somehow didn't believe Viktor would need to discuss such company affairs under our present circumstances. After the movie Sunita returned to her quarters so Karin and I made our way to the gym where, knowing there was enough room for both of us to play at keeping fit, we spent another hour or more. It wasn't far off lunchtime when we headed back to our quarters to shower, change and talk over what we might do later. I had other things on my mind, however, and said to Karin, 'That guy Viktor made up some tale about wanting to contact Earth. Now I know I have a suspicious mind but -.'

'You certainly have,' she responded, 'but go on.'

'Okay, but I can't see why he'd be wanting to do what he's claiming to do this far out from Earth.'

'I know what you mean,' she said. 'Perhaps he just doesn't like our company or it could be he wants to get into another dream world to fill out his time. We both know that feeling, don't we, Brett.'

'Sure we do but what's bugging me is that gadget he's got tucked away inside his chest. I'm going to try a second time to find out what it is.' I touched my earlobe and said, 'Orion, you tried already without success to ascertain the purpose of the device Viktor Saroyan has concealed in his upper body but as commander of this outfit I feel I ought to know what it is. I ask you to make another attempt.'

'I will do as you wish at once,' came the reply. We waited only seconds before Orion spoke again. 'I can achieve nothing unless I risk causing damage to the device and its owner. As he has a right to privacy in this respect perhaps you, or I on your behalf, should ask him directly what the device is for.'

'Fine,' I responded, 'but better if you leave it to me. Ah, wait - what's the delay time he experiences when sending and receiving messages from Earth?' It was an obvious question since I assumed his communications would, like our own, be handled by Orion.

'Viktor Saroyan has requested no communication with Earth,' came the reply. 'Do you still wish for transmission time details?'

I hesitated then replied, 'Thanks but no I don't.' I turned to Karin and asked, 'He doesn't transmit or receive through Orion even if he uses her energy field so what do we make of that?'

'It sounds as though our Viktor could be lying.'

'No, maybe he isn't – deceiving, yes, but lying – about what? He may have been in contact with Earth but as it's not through Orion I reckon I know what he has implanted in his sternum.'

'Oh, I see,' Karin said. 'You mean it's some kind of personal communications system. So he's up to something he doesn't want any of us to know about.'

'Could be he is and I intend to find out what.'

'When and where d'you propose to do that?'

'Straight after lunch,' I replied, 'when the three of you are gone and I get to corner him alone.'

Lunch was a pleasant enough affair. We all agreed on soft music and a gently flowing abstract on the dining area walls. It was easier by now to forget we were travelling through space very many times faster than anyone had done before and were so very much more distant from humanity. Arnold reflected upon the development of the hyperdrive and its implications for the future exploration of space. Karin discussed her interest in the Saturnian system with Sunita who elaborated more on the exotic chemistry of Titan, trying her best to make it sound simple as they glanced now and again at me. Viktor emphasised the forthcoming benefits of Frontier Mining's planned exploitation of Titan's resources and I referred to some of my own and Karin's experiences on Mars those few years back, before and during the time when Frontier Mining had gained temporary control there. He responded with interest amiably enough as if much of the episode was new to him but I suspected he'd had closer links with Virgil Hammond and knew more than he was willing to admit.

We'd finished eating and he was about to leave the table first when I said, 'Viktor, I need a word before you go.'

'Oh, really,' he responded, lowering back into the seat.

'Yes, really,' I said.

'We'll wander off then, shall we,' said Karin, turning to Sunita. Both left the table and pushed their plates, cups and other items into the recycling unit. Viktor's attention switched for a moment to the departing Sunita. With a polite gesture, Arnold arose and cleared his own things away before following them. Then we were alone.

'Viktor,' I said, 'that implant of yours, I presume you're in private communication with Earth. Now it may look as if I have nothing more to do on board this vessel than anyone else at present but I *am* in command of this expedition and I need to know *what* is going on. Why the secrecy – why not hold dialogue through Orion?'

A shadow of guilt crossed his face. He stared at me a while then replied, 'Some of it though not all *is* confidential company business and nothing whatsoever to do with this expedition.'

'Well considering the hours you must have needed to hold even a simple conversation this far out from Earth I'd have thought it easier to have Orion deal with such matters and request privacy there.'

'I prefer to handle these things wholly by myself but I'll tell you now, and would have done so anyway, that the rocket powered cargo vessel presently stationed with the Titan space station, the space tanker as you call it, has not been activated. It is to be abandoned altogether and those were my orders from Earth. The many years needed for its return to Mars or to Earth without the benefit of hyperdrive, and the fact that after unloading it the thing would be useless, were factors in the decision. Most of its remaining propulsive fuel might be saved to the unit accompanying us and the remainder used to power the older vessel when it is directed to leave Titan orbit and burn up in Saturn's atmosphere.'

'So that decision is in the hands of Frontier Mining is it, without reference to the International Council.'

'I believe, Commander, you will find that is now the case, as well as full control of the Titan space station, which Frontier helped to commission in the first place. Apart from overall policy on Earth what use can the International Council be for deep space operations such as ours?'

He may have been right in that respect but I was convinced there was more involved here than he was prepared to admit when I said, 'Well in future perhaps you will see fit to keep me informed of anything connected with this project and I'll decide what is and what is not important.'

'As you wish,' he breathed, getting up to leave. As the door closed I realised he hadn't dropped his things into the recycling unit. I was about to call him back but then I thought it better not to put too great a strain on a relationship that had not been too wholesome from the beginning and wasn't likely to improve. I nevertheless asked Orion to keep a closer eye on him than was necessary just for his health. So what next, I asked myself. Karin would, I knew, be busy discussing Titan with Arnold and Sunita on the control deck so maybe I'd join them or visit some virtual art gallery on Earth. There were more than enough of those to choose from. Then before dinner I would meet Karin in the gym.

***

Our next day, our second full day equivalent in space, passed without any incident worth relating other than the fact that when the sleep period arrived, Karin and I, once more warm and close together, shared our dreaming. This time it was a deeper sleep. This time our dreaming was something only she and I could ever truly understand.

We were walking - no, almost drifting together, hand in hand beneath the pale ochre sky of a Martian desert. Were we wearing space suits? I don't know but it somehow didn't matter. It was after all a dream. The dark, sheer wall of a mesa arose before us and we approached near enough to reach out and touch. We turned aside to continue along close by the rock wall then stopped to face the greater darkness of a cavern. We entered. We left the light of day and the desert behind and were passing slowly through a dark passage where a river of luminous sand flowed gently about our feet. Karin was singing and laughing as we were drawn ever onwards into an infinity of nothingness. The beams of our lights darted from side to side to reveal tiny crystals that glinted in black rock as do stars in the vastness of space. We reached out to touch but the crystal stars were cold. Then she and I were quiet because it seemed the passage might never end and all the time it was becoming almost imperceptibly narrower. At last we saw light some way ahead. A light of hope. It grew until we emerged as childlike innocents to find ourselves beneath an empty sky with lying before us an unknown box-canyon enclosed by soaring walls. We looked at one another. Karin was smiling. We continued on in awed silence to cross the level and open space until we approached the far side. There we stood before a host of pillars, each a little higher than ourselves, each topped by a cluster of dark crystals. Here was a sacred place, a vision of wonder granted to us alone. We watched light from a rising sun descend to fall upon the crystals. As it did so they began to glow, then to shine. They grew ever brighter then they blazed pulsating, colour-shifting light to bathe us in an overwhelming radiance of ecstasy. There we remained transfixed for eternal minutes. There we listened to whispered voices; voices whose words we did not comprehend. We listened and watched until the voices and the light of the crystals began slowly to fade. We remained there as the vision wavered to a golden glow. Then we slept on.

Karin stirred and I reached for her hand. 'Are you awake,' I muttered.

'Yes, Brett, I'm awake.'

'It always feels like something new, doesn't it. Always something new.'

'Always something new,' she whispered, passing an arm across me. 'As though each time we share the dream it's the very first time.'

'And now,' I said, 'now we're awake in a place where time hardly matters.'

'Not until we're hungry again,' she sighed in the darkness, 'and then I'm sure time will matter.'

***

The third full day had us sat around the lunchtime table with Arnold expressing satisfaction at the way his uprated hyperdrive system was doing its job. 'She's a beauty!' he declared. 'She's performing under these prolonged conditions exactly as specified.' What he could have done about it had it not performed as specified, I really can't imagine. He confirmed his good fortune at being among the first select few to visit Saturn and its greatest of moons in the flesh but had expressed no interest so far in descending to Titan's surface. Elated too, of course, was Sunita, who bubbled with enthusiasm at the prospect of a genuine close encounter with the hydrocarbon cornucopia that awaited us. Gesturing toward the virtual window where could be seen the space tanker, Viktor applied his praises there and appeared to believe the sole purpose of the expedition was to see how soon a self-propelled tank full of liquid methane and whatever else ended up inside it could be on its way back for processing. Like Sunita, Karin might have felt she knew Titan as thoroughly as anyone could without touching the surface but again, it was a matter of actually being there that was so important and that affected me also. When Sunita asked me, 'How do you feel, Brett, about our forthcoming encounter?'

Jeffrey Peter Clarke

'Over the moon,' I quipped.

Having adhered to the Martian day of twenty-four hours and thirty-seven minutes Orion obligingly informed us how, 'At eleven hours and fourteen minutes tomorrow I will initiate deceleration phase.'

That, as we all were aware, meant Saturn, the real Saturn, would soon after be coming into view.

60

Chapter 3
The Kingdom of Saturn

The next waking period had arrived and it will come as no surprise when I tell you that our minds were not entirely devoted to food at breakfast time. On the control deck we had a view of the sun in one of the virtual windows and found it looking little brighter than Venus when seen from Earth on a clear night. On the main display before us was showing the position and distance from our destination but we still had over two hours before deceleration was scheduled to begin, with Orion giving us a time reminder every fifteen minutes. Saturn, however, was by now visible but still a distant speck amidst a sea of stars. We agreed, and that included Viktor, not to call up a magnified image because it might spoil our real, true vision of the planet when we got up close. To kill time we discussed those other moons of Saturn outside the ring system, all explored by robot probes, in particular little Enceladus where primitive forms of life had been discovered beneath its ice bound surface. Soon enough other humans would go there. I felt it a good idea at that time to have Orion run an illustrated history of discoveries relating to Saturn and Titan beginning with Galileo; a great scientist when, in those distant days, revealing a truth did not always attract favour from those in authority. The programme was still running when Orion

61

announced, 'Deceleration will commence in fifteen minutes.'

With the history feature ended, the final countdown began. It reached thirty seconds. Then twenty. Then ten. On the big display was Saturn, growing larger second by second. As zero was announced I instinctively clutched at the arm rests of my seat as did the others, except for Arnold, but of course there was no feeling of displacement, violent or otherwise. Instead, that sensation of being at one with our vessel was much in evidence and lasted some twenty minutes during which time the display expanded to give the illusion that there was nothing between ourselves and Saturn, which now filled much of our view. Arnold gasped, 'Wow!' The rest of us, even Viktor, arose to stare in mesmerised silence. Yes, we'd all seen the great ringed planet in virtual reality but now we were witnessing the real Saturn close-up and it was truly overwhelming. Even in weak sunlight, around a hundred times fainter than at Earth, the planet glowed, as did the curving sweep of its vast and glorious ring system. For some time no one spoke then Orion announced, 'We will orbit part way about Saturn at one million kilometres and eventually catch up with Titan. This moon occupies a higher orbit at one point two million.' Orion didn't sound in the least impressed.

'How long before we actually arrive at Titan?' Karin asked her.

'We will reach five thousand kilometres distance from Titan in under one hour,' came the reply, 'then further deceleration is to take place. We will establish primary orbit at seven hundred kilometres but it is determined that when you are ready to embark upon surface exploration I establish a synthetic orbit of two hundred kilometres altitude. This is well within the atmosphere of Titan and air pressure is substantial enough to support either of the skimmers. I will descend further should you require it but I am not configured to interact with the surface.'

All five of us stared at the screen as Titan came into view around the limb of Saturn with the outer section of the ring system seeming to swing toward us. A countdown showed on the main display and although Titan grew larger by the second, no one uttered a word. During that time I assessed my own knowledge of this, Saturn's largest moon and second largest natural satellite in our Solar System. Titan is over five thousand kilometres diameter and well beyond a million kilometres from the parent planet, to which it always keeps the same face. The thick atmosphere Orion had spoken of extended up to six hundred kilometres and the human eye, unaided, could see hardly any surface features through it. Orion, of course, was able to resolve far more detail. Titan is like a layered onion with a liquid water ocean around seventy kilometres below that deep freeze organic surface and a rocky core further down still, but we'd not concern ourselves directly with either. None of the probes sent over many years to Titan had been able to drill down to liquid water but it was generally agreed that there were hydrothermal vents down there, possibly similar to those in Earth's deep seas. On Earth, of course, many different life forms had evolved in those abyssal regions. So, most people with any interest thought, why not on Titan?

Orion had slowed and the big fuzzy ball of Titan loomed large before us. We'd co-ordinated with the Titan space station, also at seven hundred kilometres above the surface and well beyond atmospheric drag. The TSS was more than a small space station; it was a somewhat angular structure consisting of an automated laboratory and crew accommodation that awaited full activation once we and our accompanying space tanker were identified to it. Docked at the station were the two shuttles intended to gather liquid methane from below. The crew section, as Arnold had earlier explained, would be accessible from Orion via an extending, flexible airlock. The one thing the TSS did not have was gravity and it had been designed accordingly but once correctly positioned within our force field this could be established in the right direction for the crew module. Might we make use of the space station quarters for rest periods? I thought not since it had been planned in the days before hyperdrive and the more than adequate facilities on Orion would render that unnecessary. I had Orion resolve the image of Titan to include wavelengths either side of the visible so that, combined with her radar, the smog all but vanished and there was Titan in all its frigid glory. There were dark plains that took up over sixty percent of the moon's surface and vast dune fields both consisting, as I had already learned, of complex organic material. There were the hills and mountains of water ice, hard as steel, and the frozen methane and ethane landforms that might melt to form rivers or glaciers flowing into hydrocarbon seas.

'Absolutely fascinating is it not,' breathed Sunita.

'Fascinating it certainly is,' agreed Arnold, 'though not very inviting I have to say.' I wondered if any enthusiasm for reaching the surface would manifest itself within the man but this so far seemed unlikely. I was nevertheless inclined to sympathise with him, I must confess. Titan did not appear inviting.

'There must be enough potential fuel down there to keep Earth and Mars supplied for the next thousand years,' I commented.

'And it's my job to see it becomes available sooner rather than later,' declared Viktor.

We'd been for some time studying the surface at varying magnifications when Orion announced, 'Brett, I have downloaded three messages; one from Earth and two from Mars. May I open these now?'

'Yes, do that,' I responded, 'but let's hear the one from Earth first.' Titan faded from view and the first image materialised before us. I had anticipated something like this and hoped none of the messages would be unduly long. First was the newly-elected President of the United American States together with a small group of officials in attendance. A hard-faced woman of about fifty with short dark hair parted in the middle, she offered us, as she put it, her "heartfelt congratulations" as the first humans to venture beyond the orbit of Mars and, "what a historic moment this is and what it must mean for our species as true citizens of space." I wish I could have told her how little we actually had to do as cosseted passengers of Orion but I guess she would not have wanted to hear that. While she was talking I recognised one of the faces of a guy standing close to her – an associate of Virgil Hammond from the rigged conference held those few years back on the Isaac Newton space station above Mars. I didn't know his name but it appeared Frontier Mining really had gained a degree of respectability.

When she'd finished her off-the-shelf eulogies and faded out, the second relay materialised and this was an altogether more welcome one for Karin and myself because it was Joe Van Allen. Joe was sitting in his office and would you believe, I could see that ancient clock of his ticking away close by on the desk. 'Hi, Brett, hi, Karin,' he began, 'and you other three out there with those two reprobates. I'm almost jealous of you all so I hope you make good use of your time. I'll make sure there's plenty of bourbon around here for when you're back home so don't take any risks, and Brett, that means you. Meanwhile, Orion's been keeping me informed of all that matters so I'm sure you'll return as fit and healthy as when you left.' Joe raised a hand then was gone.

Third to gaze down upon us was the smiling face of Amalia Barbosa on the Isaac Newton space station. As Mars' official ambassador to Earth, though she seldom went there, she also wished us a productive and interesting visit to Titan. 'When you return,' she ended, 'I'll drop down to Number One and join you all for a welcome drink. Meanwhile, Joe is keeping me up to date with everything.'

Those messages from Mars must have taken a good deal more than an hour to reach us and that from Earth a while longer. But I was now to find more use for myself and ordered Orion to take control of and place the older cargo vessel, the so-called space tanker that Viktor had proposed should be sent to a fiery doom in Saturn's atmosphere, into a higher orbit. She's not for destruction just yet, I concluded, but I had no special reason in mind for making that decision other than to have it mine rather than Viktor's. Plenty of unwanted space probes and satellites had ended up that way since the outer planets were ideal for garbage disposal or anything else you didn't want to leave hanging about when it became useless. We stood to watch the tanker's manoeuvring jets fire, turn her around and have her a respectable distance from everything, particularly ourselves, before her main rocket engine lit up to move her ahead and upwards against the stars. She'd remain in that higher orbit, which meant she'd gradually fall behind us, until I'd had final thoughts over her fate. I noted Viktor's expression; he wasn't too happy that I'd seen fit to implement a decision over something owned by Frontier. I next had Orion decouple our own companion vessel, the accompanying space tanker, and move her a short distance away from us until needed. We watched her drift back about a hundred metres then I turned to the others and said, 'Okay, we have our respective programmes to follow so let's go and eat and then decide who does what and when.'

That suggestion didn't need a vote so to the dining area we headed. Once we were seated Arnold said, 'Now we're arrived I wish to make further checks and final assessment with my own equipment of all Orion's systems associated with the power core but this will not interfere in any way with her functioning.'

'Sure,' I replied, 'we know that's what you were here for so she's all yours, as long as you make the results of your work available to me in a language I and others can understand.'

'I'll do my best,' he smiled. 'Oh, and I would also like to go aboard and look around the TSS if that is at all possible.'

I noticed Viktor's expression again; it seemed he didn't go with that idea either. Even less did he appear to like it when Sunita said, 'Yes and I would be interested also to see how laboratory facilities there match up with those we have on Orion.'

'Fine,' I said, 'then we should check out the TSS before I have Orion drop closer to the surface where we can deploy one of our skimmers.'

Viktor drew sharp breath and said, 'May I suggest I enter our station first before full gravity is applied. It was designed to function in a no gravity situation and I'm concerned that damage may be caused, particularly in the laboratory if various items are not correctly arranged and secured. A low level gravity to begin with would be of some assistance. For two hours, perhaps, whilst I make an assessment.'

It seemed at the time a reasonable proposition since it *was* Frontier's own project and Viktor ought to know more than any of us what was involved there. 'Okay,' I agreed, 'I'll have Orion apply minimal gravity; say, ten percent of our own. I'll have her manoeuvre close enough to the laboratory unit to achieve that and I'll have the extendable airlock connected and leave you to get on with whatever you have in mind.'

'Then I,' said Viktor, 'will remain over in my laboratory and return here before gravity is lost. But I trust when the samples are acquired an additional quantity will be made available for usage over there.'

'I imagine that will not be a problem,' responded Sunita, looking at me for approval. 'I am sure there will be sufficient material.'

'No problem,' I confirmed. The skimmer, I knew, could easily grab hold of and package two samples of everything in her containers because small quantities were all we needed. With that Viktor left us and Karin asked, 'What's he going to do with any samples – he's no scientist, or is he?'

'I ran an additional check on him through Orion not long after we boarded,' I answered. 'He's taken precautions to stop anyone delving too deeply and that, I'm certain, will be Frontier's doing. It does seem, though, he's undertaken some research work and that's why he wants to get those samples into his own laboratory. I can't see that doing any harm so long as we don't let him loose in our own.'

'No, please,' said Sunita, raising her hands, 'not in our lab. It is scheduled for my work only.'

Karin asked, 'Have you decided on a time to take one of the surface skimmers down?'

Her question implied that only I was cleared to operate one of those things and that was true, although it was little more than a technicality. Anyone allocated voice control could do so and Karin, as had I, gained full experience in the simulator on Mars.

'We'll go during our next work period,' I answered; the next work period being the equivalent of tomorrow. 'What we haven't decided yet is who will go down there with me first unless you both wish to.' Of the two skimmers on board; both could be directed from Orion but one would be set by for emergencies. Either could hold four people but I wasn't happy initially about taking more than one passenger. Nevertheless I imagined Karin and Sunita would be equally enthusiastic to see the surface close up, Sunita in particular until she said, 'Brett, if you are to go during our next work period you must take Karin first. Now we are in orbit I need to have Orion scan a number of surface areas in detail and get on with some of my work in our own laboratory before leaving the ship. I will wish also to examine the samples you are to collect before deciding where I need to go.'

Well that solved one problem and suited Karin well enough but I was not about to forgo such an opportunity any more than those two and it was my responsibility to be first down there anyway with whoever else. The samples, too, would be fresher than anything so far carried back to Earth by automated probes. Did we anticipate any danger? No, we were sure we knew enough about Titan not to worry about that. I say "we" because during our so-called working periods I had done what I should have done even before leaving Mars; I had clued myself up a little on some aspects of Titan.

Orion had moved into position and connected to the TSS when Viktor, having rechecked remotely in advance conditions on board the laboratory unit, made his way through the airlock connected to his pride and joy wearing only his crew suit. I didn't doubt he'd be planning on how soon he might begin getting the space tanker, still loitering behind us, filled with liquid Methane and on its way back to Earth. I was convinced by now that Viktor saw our research work at Titan as an impediment to Frontier Mining. His sole purpose was in demonstrating to the powers back on Earth, with a full consignment of methane, what Frontier could achieve. The tanker was not designed to interface directly with Titan's surface but the two rocket powered shuttles presently attached to the TSS, each making three visits, would serve to fill her to capacity. Anyway, the rest of us would carry on and leave him to go about whatever he needed to until our late period meal. Viktor might or might not come back over to join us as his subsequent request to increase gravity could mean he intended to stay onboard the station for some time.

***

We were into the next work period before I summoned Viktor back to Orion. Having spent the rest period in his laboratory and crew quarters he joined us for breakfast where I asked him, 'How is everything over there?'

'All is as I would have wished,' he answered, 'there are no problems I'm pleased to say and everything of importance is secured for use throughout the station with or without gravity.'

We discussed at length the various aspects of Titan, her bizarre geography and atmosphere, with Viktor at least a part of the conversation until our meals were finished. He said little else after that then rose from his seat without further comment.

'Viktor seems to have much on his mind,' commented Arnold as the man in question left, so we presumed, for his quarters.

'Scooping up methane,' said Karin, 'is all he's got on his mind and he's left his bits and pieces here on the table for us to scoop up instead.'

'It's not the first time,' I muttered.

'I'd still like to see that laboratory of his,' said Arnold, 'so when you're back from the surface -.'

'When we're back from the surface,' I assured him, 'I reckon we'll all take a look, especially Sunita as she'll better understand what he's been up to with the samples we'll have given him, though strictly speaking it *is* his territory.'

'I will look forward to it anyway,' Sunita smiled.

'Back on Mars,' Karin said, 'he was almost telling us what a great place the space station would be to stay but it seems he's changed his mind.'

'Maybe Frontier helped him,' I remarked.

'Viktor is in sole charge of the shuttles for siphoning up liquid methane and transferring it to the cargo vessel, isn't he,' Karin said. 'Could he begin those operations while we're down there, or even sooner?'

'Not without my permission,' I answered. 'The new tanker is supposed to be under our control through Orion until we're almost done with our surface work in case we get in each other's way. She's drifting loose at present outside our force field but there's nothing I can do about that while we're attached to the space station.'

'He'll be onto you about our schedule, won't he,' said Arnold.

'Maybe he will,' I shrugged, 'but it's time Karin and I did as we planned; so if you will excuse us.' We left them and headed off to our quarters to get ourselves ready and once there I said to Karin, 'Now don't you laugh but I've done a bit of catching up work on Titan so I have a better idea what I'm looking at. When we're on our way you can check me out with what's going on in case there are a few things I overlooked.'

She stared at me open-mouthed, saying, 'Catching up, Brett – have you really?'

'I have - er some, a bit as I say, but you're the expert, that's for sure.'

She looked at me with those big blue eyes and said, 'Alright, you can tell me what you've learned and I'll try to explain a little more as we go, but you'll want to play at steering the skimmer like a little boy once we're down there. I know perfectly well how you prefer to drive things even when they're designed to save normal people the trouble.'

'That's true,' I muttered. 'I seldom trust machines unless I have no option.'

'Alright,' she grinned, 'but you'd better concentrate on doing that. I don't want us crashing into anything.'

A short time later I authorised Orion to cut physical connections with the TSS, separate from it and descend to two hundred kilometres above the surface of Titan while running final checks on the skimmer we intended to use. Arnold and Sunita, joined by Viktor, watched us suit up and step through the airlock into the spacious dorsal compartment where the two skimmers were located. Suiting up was a necessary precaution even I accepted though the skimmers were hermetically sealed. They were adapted for use on Titan – as much to keep the inside atmosphere in as to keep the toxic outside atmosphere out. The airlock slid shut and we boarded the allocated skimmer, a comfortable enough helicopter vehicle with good all around visibility through the armaplast bubble canopy. Titan was at that time some way into the sunlit side of Saturn so there would be days of modest illumination as well as that shone out in any direction by the skimmer's powerful lamps. The skimmer would, of course, record everything we saw and more, and would relay it back to Orion.

'May I monitor both your physiological responses as we progress?' asked the skimmer in a somewhat metallic, none gender-specific voice.

'No you may not!' I replied sharply. 'I feel absolutely fine so just do as you're told and get us down there.' You know already how I resented being scrutinised by machines. Karin had little concern over such matters and said, 'Yes, you can keep a check on mine.'

We watched the readout on the panel close outside our canopy as it indicated declining airlock pressure, then a section of the hull above was sliding open. With a smooth humming our blades began to rotate. At that altitude we'd have no need of our jets to lift us clear of Orion as atmospheric density was already well above sufficient and at the surface would be over fifty percent higher than that of Earth. 'She's programmed to take us to the surface,' I told Karin, 'but once we're there I still intend to take over.'

'I'll try not to panic, Brett, dear,' she replied as our blades picked up speed and we began to rise.

We were both aware, of course, that the skimmer would override manual control instantly to avoid obstacles no matter who was in the pilot's seat. We would also be closely monitored by Orion. She'd put out three satellites for that very purpose so we'd always be under observation and warned of any dangers ahead whether we or the skimmer had spotted them or not. One thing we understood from the very beginning; we'd not be able to leave the skimmer. Because of the relatively much higher temperature of our insulated suits, almost anything we touched or trod upon down there would melt or even vaporise at once. What appeared to be solid ground might become a lethal quicksand.

We lifted away and drifted aside from the mother vessel, peering through the canopy of our skimmer at the vista of Titan's equatorial region opening out below us, clearer than it had been from our higher orbit. As with Saturn, we'd seen it all recreated from images sent back over the decades by probes and satellites but now we were about to reach out and physically touch the surface; or at least our skimmer was. Yes, Karin and I would be the first humans to land there and Titan awaited!

We were descending through the atmosphere when, as we moved further from Orion, Karin began to question me on what we were seeing. 'Are you sure this is the right time for a memory test?' I asked.

'Yes it is since you're not in control of anything yet. You should know by now what you're looking at so don't make excuses.'

I sensed even then she was trying to affect a sense of normality. I guessed she was feeling uneasy, but then who wouldn't be in this most novel of situations. One of the few things I'd managed to check out in our journey across space included what was going on from top to bottom of that crazy, mainly nitrogen atmosphere we'd now entered but that was nearly all of what I'd managed. Karin, of course, understood a great deal more than most people and Sunita was the committed specialist in organics, so I didn't dare get too involved.

'The haze we just passed through,' she asked at one point, 'was that a part of your homework?'

'Oh, definitely,' I replied with outwardly cheerful confidence as, staring beyond the canopy, I tried hard to remember more of what I'd earlier studied. 'Tholin haze it's called, right?' The atmosphere cleared further. Our view had improved greater by far than it had been from our initial orbit.

'Yes, go on,' she urged.

'Okay, tholins are complex hydrocarbons formed high in the atmosphere when ultraviolet light and cosmic rays strike carbon-rich molecules like methane or ethane and have them combine in all sorts of ways I don't care to think about. Then as they get heavier they all drift down to the surface to make things even more difficult to figure out. Okay teacher, how am I doing?'

Karin stared at me with a contrived expression of amazement, saying, 'Well it's not too bad a start.'

I didn't want to be over smug about it because if you've ever looked into organic chemistry you'll have discovered, as I had earlier, how dauntingly complicated a subject it is.

'We're dropping through more layers of chemical haze,' said Karin as we peered about.

'And I bet these clouds we're about to pass through,' I remarked casually, 'are methane and ethane with maybe a touch of ammonia.'

'Oh, well done,' she breathed as we gazed further into the distance.

The surface itself appeared much clearer as we continued down so the interrogation, somewhat to my relief, had to take a back seat. The screen before us displayed our location with named features but this I dimmed down. We looked about in silence but witnessing what we were heading toward didn't cheer me up any. Beneath us spread a forbidding landscape, a sombre vista of weird dreams, or was it nightmares when I considered the toxic content of the atmosphere and the profound cold at the surface. To our left, light glinted upon a river of liquid methane that entered a vast lake edged by a rising land of dark organic dunes, a landscape that arose higher, becoming brighter in places where it consisted of hills and mountains of water ice frozen steel-hard. Close below us drifted scattered groups of small, pale methane clouds, in form if not in substance or colour, not unlike those on Earth. With a twist of imagination we might have been gazing down at some way-out region on the home planet on a dismal, twilight day in deep winter. I glanced up to observe Saturn, now a ghostly image as if seen through a pale, ochre-tinted mist. We ceased descending at fifty metres above what looked like a deep brownish coloured dry area of land. 'I await your further instructions,' announced the skimmer.

'I'll take hands on control,' I answered, and with that the control stick slid forward to within easy reach.

By now we were fully engrossed by what lay below and ahead of us. 'Incredible,' I muttered. 'What an incredible place this is.'

'Incredible,' repeated Karin. 'Don't know about you, Brett, but it makes me think of some vast, badly lit stage.'

I knew what she meant by that and it would have to be the kind of stage waiting for a dark tragedy.

'A few say it's Earth-like, don't they,' she said. 'I wonder how most of those people would feel if they were actually here instead of sitting somewhere cosy to look at processed pictures.'

I did sympathise with her comments, though. It had never quite struck me when looking at virtual images how eerie the place was. 'So where d'you figure we head first?' I asked as we peered about.

'Well as we have to collect initial ground and liquid samples for Sunita,' she answered, 'and for dear Viktor, we may as well begin with the dry area directly below us.'

Being this close to the surface, visibility was good enough for us to see almost as far as the horizon when looking across the flat lake and our own lights flooded the area for some way ahead of us. I took the skimmer down to rest on what, according to our sensors, seemed to be a slightly soft, coarse-grained sand.

'We did it!' I declared. 'We touched ground. Pity we can't drink to it.' Our skis, you will have realised, were as cold as the exterior and kept the main body of our skimmer clear of the ground.

'Yes, we did it didn't we,' Karin responded, though with less elation than I might have expected.

'We'll go down in history,' I assured her as our external scoops, equally cold, were activated.

'D'you think so, Brett?' she queried. 'Until today the journey's been an almost routine affair and I think that's how many people, particularly on Earth, will continue to look at it.'

She was right of course; immense distance or no, we'd travelled in comfort without any of those risks faced by the first explorers setting out to the Moon or to Mars. We sat there a while in silence, feeling a slight shudder as our scoops took in and sealed around a kilogram in each of two inert containers well to our rear. Glancing at our screen I noted the skimmer was doing a basic analysis on a small part of this ground material and already displayed an incomprehensible, at least to me, list of complex hydrocarbon formulae that would now be beamed up to Orion. I imagined how absorbed Sunita would be when downloading this data. 'What's most of this stuff made of?' I asked Karin as we completed this first part of our operation.

'Well since you ask,' she replied, peering at the screen as I lifted us clear, 'it looks like a varying mixture of polycyclic aromatic hydrocarbons. I'm sure Sunita will explain all about it in greater detail if you ask her nicely.'

'Explain all about - er, right, but I wouldn't want to take up her valuable time just yet. Where next?'

'To that river estuary we spotted a way over to our north,' she replied, 'then a couple of samples from the lake itself. Sunita will want to analyse those as well but when you bring her down here she'll no doubt be more specific as to exactly where you have to go. She'll certainly want to check out one of those cryovolcano areas where liquid water is rising to the surface from deep underground.'

I took us up some two hundred metres, hovered a while so we could look all about, then headed in the required direction before speaking again. 'You'll be with us, though won't you. If you wanted you could pilot the skimmer yourself. You'd simply tell it what to do and I'd just sit in the back and admire the scenery?' She offered no reply. The suggestion was a bit pointless, I guess, but I wanted to lighten her mood. I sensed Karin's usual spirit of easy-going enthusiasm was giving way to a degree of unease. This was something I'd not expected even under our present circumstances so I asked, 'Are you feeling okay right now?'

'Yes, Brett, I'm okay but I'm not sure I want to come down here a second time. I'm sorry but I'll find plenty to occupy myself with back on board Orion, including an overall analysis of our journey so far.'

'But why, when you were so keen earlier? And you'll have plenty of time for any other work on our way back home.'

As that other-worldly scenery drifted by she turned to me and replied, 'I don't know; it's amazing to think we've travelled such a very long way and we're the first humans to visit Titan but I – I feel, I feel somehow we ought not to be here. There's an intensity, a sort of brooding intensity about the place I cannot put properly into words.'

'It's not like you to talk that way,' I said.

'I know, Brett and I really *am* sorry. It sounds stupid – no, thoroughly irrational but it's – it's as if Titan is waiting - but for what I have no idea. It's as if - as if it somehow is aware of us being here.'

'But earlier probes have not detected any signs of life if that's what you mean; you've said so yourself.'

'That's true, Brett, they haven't. Nothing could possibly live on the surface here, could it.' She thought for some moments then added, 'Forget I said what I did, please.'

What Karin had just disclosed had me wondering a little but I said nothing more for a while. I understood her feelings in a way, though; Mars we had colonised and adapted to but never, I thought, could humanity do so on Titan. The skimmer would have recorded our conversations but maybe that was something I could deal with later. Aware once again of the sound of our rotors I continued on at the same height under the spectral image of Saturn, towards our next set-down. Soon we were approaching open water. Water did I say! Well that's sure what it looked like even though it wasn't. It was part of a vast body, mainly of methane called, as our display informed us, the Kraken Sea. It stretched towards the north polar region and we were at its southern end. Over to our right was the river we'd spotted from high above so I slowed the skimmer and descended over the estuary. 'We'll grab a couple of bites out of this,' I said, 'then we'll head further out to where it's clearer for a dose of liquid, okay?'

'Yes, let's do that,' Karin replied. I dropped us down to an area of small islets set amid rippling methane that glinted eerily in our lights as a thousand winking eyes. Wisps of pale mist drifted here and there, coiling and uncoiling like spectral figures searching for who knew what as they hugged the wet ground.

'It's only methane vapour,' said Karin.

The skimmer, her skis part resting on this frigid goo, soon confirmed the required samples were taken up and secured. 'We require no visual analysis at this time,' I said to the skimmer as incomprehensible organic formulae began to download before me. I don't think even Sunita, had she been with us, would have been interested at that point anyway. As the screen cleared we lifted off and set out further from the fragmented coastline. Minutes later I let us down slowly, and allowed the lower part of the skimmer to settle into the liquid which began to bubble all about us due to the vanishingly small amount of heat retained by the insulated shell of the skimmer. Had there been sufficient warmth on the outside of our small vessel it would have caused the methane to boil and surround us with a dense mist, but now it began to calm. 'We're also the very first to go sailing on Titan,' I remarked, 'but I don't plan on taking a dip just yet.'

'Sailing, yes Brett, so we are,' Karin responded in a low voice as we gazed out over the lake.

The liquid samples were taken and confirmed as secure but such was the bizarre novelty of our situation I wanted to stay there a while longer. I was aware how we rose and fell gently like a boat on water, something I hadn't experienced in reality since my earlier life on Earth so I held us there longer than I ought to have, almost forgetting how Karin might feel. Then - 'Hey, it's raining!' I exclaimed. A few random splashes hit but soon the armaplast canopy that contained us was spattered by a kind of slow-motion squall. It consisted of large blobs rather than drops that shimmered and sparkled in our lights like jewels as they swooped through the air toward us. But instead of running down in streaks like proper rain, the stuff evaporated as soon as it touched our protective shell. Then the squall passed as quickly as it had come. I'd heard Titan had rain but that didn't stop me being surprised. The sea all about us billowed gently. It caused the skimmer to sway back and forth. I was peering aside, fascinated, when Karin pointed ahead and exclaimed, 'Brett, look!'

Something moved on the liquid some way from us. It was getting closer, darting from side to side as it approached, illuminated by our lights. It looked to be no more than a half-metre across, a kind of pale, rock shaped form, bubbling, fizzing as it weaved around, came and went, bobbing up and down as it eventually passed some way to our right. 'What the hell is that?' I muttered with my hand on the control stick.

Karin peered across and said, 'Brett, I think I see what it is. Shall we lift off from here – please.'

'Okay, right now,' I said as the blades above us picked up speed. 'I reckon it was no more a chunk of dissolving methane.' I hoped to sound reassuringly knowledgeable as we lifted clear.

'Yes,' she responded, 'that's all it was. I'd expect it to fizz like that if it was giving off other gasses.'

'Just ask me any time,' I grinned.

We had one more task to complete that day should it prove possible – recovery of the very first human artefact to set down upon this world, way back in the year two thousand and five - the Huygens lander. It was famous for that reason, like the Wright Flyer, like Sputnik One or Apollo Eleven. We had its original location as ten degrees, fifty seven south by one nine two thirty-three west, close to another expanse of sea. It had drifted from its original position through crustal movement but Orion had fed the skimmer with its estimated present location. I wondered if the thing might be part buried as we sped along at a hundred metres altitude. Once descending to hover over the designated area we scanned the surface until the Huygens' presence was confirmed, then I took us slowly down with our lamps directed to the spot.

'There it is!' Karin exclaimed. 'There, Brett, just to our left!'

'Wow, we have it!' I exclaimed on setting eyes upon what had to be a real treasure. Below us the ground appeared a kind of mushy orange though our sensors indicated it to have a reasonably firm surface. Scattered all about were pebbles that Karin, eyeing our display, confirmed from that and from the lander's own reports during those far off days as granite-hard water ice with a hydrocarbon coating. I swung us around and peered out at what looked for those first moments like just a grit-covered chunk of smooth metal. Then I saw it was a disk part covered in a layer of brownish organic ash, some of which was dispersed by the wash of our rotors. 'Okay,' I said, 'let's see if we can get the thing out of there.' I was aware that in Titan's gravity, fourteen percent that of Earth's, the probe would weigh only around forty-five kilograms but at little short of three metres diameter it would be almost the maximum size our grappling gear could handle, and we had to avoid causing any damage to this most precious artefact. As the skimmer was already programmed for what had to be a delicate operation I was, with lingering reservations, willing to let her go ahead on her own. We watched on our display as the skis retracted and the two metal arms deployed beneath us where they opened out to their full width of three metres. The skimmer lowered and the two mechanical arms reached down to engage. 'Easy does it,' I muttered as the right side arm obtained a secure hold. On the left it was not so easy because the arm there needed to push some way beneath the ground before the skimmer registered a firm grip. 'We have her,' I breathed as our rotors picked up speed and we began slowly to rise with the Huygens lander secured in our grasp.

'We're recovering a piece of immense historical importance,' said Karin as we watched loose material spill from our prize. 'I can only hope it isn't damaged after all the time down here.'

'She looks okay as far as I can tell, so now we get her up there with our sample containers to Sunita in the lab and Viktor's share to the space station.' I ordered the skimmer to take us back. She would inform Orion of our return and we would soon rendezvous at the pre-determined two hundred kilometres altitude. With nothing to do for a while I peered down at that bizarre, cold hell of a landscape then turned to Karin. 'D'you still feel there might be some kind of life down there; that's how I interpret what you said a while back?'

'Look, Brett, I don't know what came over me. I was being irrational but I think it's because Titan is such a – I can think of no other word for it – such an utterly hostile place. Some people, even in the time of the lander we just rescued, suggested it might be a better world to live than Mars. How could anyone *possibly* think so even in those days.'

'I agree and I don't see anything other than research stations in orbit but who knows, someone may get to love the place; it takes all sorts.'

'Yes, it certainly does and we were taught, weren't we, how people once had such reservations about Mars. But, Brett, I've changed my mind; I won't let Titan get at me - I will after all join you and Sunita during whatever Orion decides is tomorrow since time has become rather meaningless.'

'It's not meaningless according to my stomach,' I assured her as we ascended to pre-planned altitude and Orion came into view.

'Nor mine I suppose. Pity alcohol isn't available; I could do with a drop of something stronger than fruit juice or coffee.'

'Yeah,' I breathed, 'maybe I'll have a word with Orion since we're the best of pals.'

Before our skimmer took her place back on board the mother ship she released the Huygens lander. Orion sent out a couple of bots to guide this most important relic into an externally accessed compartment on the space tanker where it would be cosseted for the time being. I'd decided that the tanker and not Orion would return it to Earth after the former had discharged the agreed portion of its cargo on Mars. The bots would first remove much of the material attached to the Huygens, some of which would end up with Sunita for examination in our lab. Those same bots would transfer the samples allocated to Viktor Saroyan over to the space station once we'd returned to seven hundred kilometres altitude. We were soon back inside Orion where our suits and the skimmer herself were sterilised as rules demanded; rules with which in this case I was happy to comply.

All of us gathered for dinner where discussion centred on what Karin and I had done, what we'd seen and how she and I felt about Titan. Arnold and Sunita, the latter in particular, were much interested but for once it was Viktor who paid his share of attention and asked questions, mainly about the lakes and seas. We cleared our cluttered table, yes, even Viktor managed it on this occasion, then we made our way to the control deck where we talked further. We next agreed to watch another old-time movie on the main display; this time a twentieth century science fiction classic. Strange I thought as we sat there, how people in those days believed humans could travel to or aliens could invade Earth from another planet millions of light years distant.

For the next sleep period Karin and I decided we'd leave off dreaming and take a deeper, longer rest. We agreed a return to programmed dreaming was perhaps what we'd do on our way back home.

***

On our third nominated day at Titan we awoke to the soft yet compelling voice of Orion. She sensed we had overslept. Before the usual morning procedures I asked Karin, 'Are you still keen on going down there again?'

'I'm not going back on my word,' she smiled, 'so come along now, let's get ourselves ready.'

The five of us were seated together for breakfast. During this work period I would take Sunita down for her first visit to the surface of Titan and Karin would be with us for her second. Sunita had to acquire more specific samples and, aided by the dining area display, briefed me on the places we were to check out, including what Karin had referred to on our first trip as a cryovolcano. We'd seen such features on movies sent back from Titan by drones but this one had been out of sight and only spotted from above quite recently. It did sound interesting but I held back from questioning her over it as there were other matters to discuss. We also might be dropping by one of those areas where a mid twenty-first century lander had ended up but failed to relay any information. It seemed somebody on Earth wanted it back to find out what had gone wrong. Karin had no specific project in mind other than to study what Sunita would be doing and I guess she was still determined to shake off that fear she had experienced earlier. Viktor expressed his intention to work through his period onboard the Titan space station and I had to remind him that he'd be without gravity while Orion was taking the skimmer down to lower orbit. 'So I'll have to put up with that until you return,' he informed me. 'I have everything arranged as needed.' He shrugged, eyed Sunita momentarily then left us. The prospect of floating about in the TSS would, anyhow have been a part of his agenda and training. Arnold having already made clear his wish to look over Viktor's laboratory would await our return also. Arnold had still expressed no desire to visit Titan's surface and made it clear, when the subject was raised, that virtual visits were all he wanted. A short while later the three of us suited up and, followed by Arnold, headed for the skimmer bay. Viktor was by then nowhere in evidence so we assumed, as the flexible airlock was still in place, that he'd already made it over to his own laboratory and quarters.

Orion uncoupled from the space station and made her descent. Once at two hundred kilometres altitude we cleared the mother ship and the skimmer was on her way down to a pre-determined height. Only now, only on my second visit to this sombre realm, did I really appreciate Karin's earlier sentiments. Yes, I also regarded Titan as a vast, living stage-set with the ethereal image of Saturn hanging above and for a time I found myself wondering, irrational as it seemed, if we *were* the sole actors. I gazed out at the forlorn landscape, thinking if I might incorporate it with my own fantasies as I had with those on Mars, then I dismissed the idea entirely. Still, I could allow myself a short while to fantasise because Sunita's desired locations were already programmed into the skimmer. It made sense to let it find its own way to each in turn as there would be more opportunity for conversation time with my two passengers.

'Not driving today?' came Karin's voice from behind and I snapped back into stark reality as we sped along some ten metres above the surface.

'I'm taking a well-earned break,' was my only comment. Otherwise Sunita and Karin did most of the talking and I part listened as each elaborated upon some of the features we saw about us.

Our first sample pick-up was from another estuary, the outlet of a meandering methane-ethane stream rather than a river, emerging from a deep gully, this some way into the northern hemisphere. It looked to me thereabouts like a mainly dry area with the kind of brownish sand we'd encountered on that first visit, but it was material from just below the shallow, bubbling liquid Sunita wanted. This was done quickly enough as our skimmer hovered close above and began to display her analysis, which Sunita studied for some moments. We were lifting off when my earlobe pinged and Orion informed me, 'Brett, Viktor Saroyan has taken full control of the cargo vessel from within the Titan space station and he has initiated pre-programmed activation of the shuttles to obtain and load methane. I am unable to intervene as these units are not under our jurisdiction.'

'But the cargo vessel, the space tanker, *is* under our jurisdiction,' I said. Awaiting Orion's response, I ordered the skimmer to stop and hover.

'That was so but it is no longer,' she replied. 'Since the cargo vessel was decoupled in orbit Viktor Saroyan was able to override any previous programming and to access full command.'

'Dammit,' I muttered, 'I should have seen that coming.'

'What's happening?' asked Karin.

'What's happening,' I answered, 'is that Viktor is now able to go ahead with the transfer of -.' As if on cue a glare appeared suddenly overhead. We looked up to see a rocket-powered winged vehicle crossing that part of the sky where Saturn loomed and descending on its way to the west of us.

'It's one of the shuttles from the space station isn't it,' said Karin as the glow vanished below the horizon.

'Yes it is one of the shuttles heading down to fill up with methane and that's exactly what Viktor is authorised to do.' The shuttle was also equipped with rotor blades similar to our own and would deploy these in order to hover and take up its liquid cargo. Viktor Saroyan was going it alone without a by your leave.

'Then must we now return to Orion?' Sunita asked.

I thought for some moments then replied, 'Maybe not – no, the whole process he's initiated up there will be automated and I'll not be able to stop it unless by force. More to the point I'm not sure what justification I could offer for doing that.'

'Are we then to continue as we were?' asked Karin as I allowed the skimmer to fly on.

'We may as well.' But as I spoke I had it in mind that I'd give that guy Saroyan a hard time as soon as we were back on our ship for his lack of co-operation in not keeping me informed. Then I had the skimmer speed up further so we could continue with our own programme. We next flew south toward the equator and were passing over a dark, rock-strewn plain when the skimmer began to slow. It was at this point Karin leaned forward to ask, 'Brett, in your studies of Titan's features I hope you've learned why there are so few craters here because the one we're approaching is quite rare.'

'Er, yes, as it happens,' I responded, 'it's because of erosion and because some of them get recycled over the ages by a kind of plate tectonics. Anything else you need to know while I'm not too busy?'

'Oh, we *are* doing well,' she said. Karin sounded more at ease than on our previous trip and was actually smiling, together with Sunita, at my modest verbal offering. Not actually ground-breaking, if you'll pardon the pun, because it was one of those things anyone with an interest in Titan would probably know about anyway. Ahead of us arose a low, curving wall, less than two metres high, that proved to be the rim of a smallish crater. 'We don't have a precise location here for digging anything up, do we,' I said.

'No,' replied Sunita, 'I need to see where we can best take our samples. From inside the crater wall would be preferable.'

I decided it might be better if I took over our skimmer and called for the control stick. The crater, around forty metres across, looked an almost perfect circle and contained within it a jumbled layer of white material that rose to a two metre high peak of sorts at its centre. It looked to me like some kind of roughly carved monument but to what I had no idea. With the skimmer feeding back ground information we dropped low to move slowly over Sunita's chosen area. Sunita peered down until seeing what she considered a suitable spot for gathering material and said, 'Just here, Brett, if you can.'

'No problem,' I assured her as with our rotors slowing, the skimmer eased into position. The skimmer shook slightly as the scoops reached down to accomplish their task and minutes later confirmed our latest samples were taken.

'The crater is filled with solid water and methane ice,' explained Sunita as the skimmer began her basic analysis of the stuff we'd collected. Sunita, with Karin peering over her shoulder, started to comment upon what was appearing on our screen. I took one look at it and said, 'Interesting formation in the middle of the crater, though, isn't it.'

'Oh, very interesting,' agreed Sunita, switching her attention momentarily from the screen.

'The impact must have caused frozen water below the ground to melt then to burst out and refreeze straight away,' added Karin.

With the crater samples secured we lifted off and flew on to Sunita's next goal, again at high speed with the skimmer once more in control and her engine an ever reassuring purr. We passed over the equator and some way into the southern hemisphere where we approached a spectacular range of high hills, some cracked and dislocated and rising like stark, jagged teeth against a sombre sky. Then another distraction, a second rocket glow in the sky, this time heading north-west. I took control again, slowed and this time turned the skimmer about so we could watch the shuttle descend and disappear below the horizon. 'Okay,' I said, 'but we still carry on as before.' Orion was now keeping me fully informed of shuttle movements through my ear lobe communications.

The three of us peered ahead at those pallid hills as Sunita announced, 'What we are seeing is made mainly of water ice, but as in the crater it is frozen hard as granite. I would like samples of this ice, please, Brett.'

Granite hard was the way I was feeling about Viktor Saroyan when I said, calmly, 'Sure, we can drill out a couple of chunks.' I continued in control of our skimmer, taking us further up, past precipitously sloping walls of dark-streaked, tormented ice, until we hovered close above one of the less jagged hills that rose to a height of almost eight hundred metres. There we settled gently onto a relatively flat, slightly shelving surface.

'That is wonderful,' declared Sunita and I could only admire her enthusiasm as we began to carry out this next operation. The cylindrical drill ran with the high-pitched whine that sang through the skimmer and through our own bodies. Perched where we were for twenty or so minutes above those chaotic ranges accorded us the kind of views that on Earth or parts of Mars would have been spectacular. Spectacular they were here also but menacing, almost shocking in the grim aspect they presented. 'Nice view,' I remarked.

'I see from the display our next location is not so far away,' Sunita remarked when the drill ended its task and retracted.

'Less than seventy kilometres,' I confirmed, letting the skimmer take over. With the samples stowed, we flew on, passing over peaks that rose up, taunting, threatening, as if wishing to seize and drag us down into frozen oblivion. But soon we were to witness perhaps the most remarkable of all the sights we would encounter on this most alien of worlds. As I already mentioned, this was a recent discovery, never visited close up by a drone, maybe because it hadn't been around for very long, and that was why Sunita had chosen it. We descended until entering a deep, meandering valley between the ice walls, dropping lower, ever lower into Hadean depths. We slowed until only some ten meters above its shadowed and forbidding surface where writhing coils of vapour scurried speedily by in the same direction as ourselves, as if in fear, over some kind of iced-over hydrocarbon rubble. The skimmer confirmed the presence of a strong wind but not one to compromise our progress since it was flowing with rather than against us. I resisted the temptation to ask either of my passengers what the stuff below us might be made of since it probably wouldn't mean much and our skimmer was too high to perform an analysis. That grim valley was a place where I had no desire to hang about and I was feeling concerned over Karin who I imagined must wish for nothing more than to be back on board Orion. Even Sunita remained silent for a time, peering wide-eyed from side to side as we flew on. The valley twisted left, the skimmer was reducing speed and then we saw it. Ahead of us, bursting out of the ground, was a fountain, some twenty or so metres high!

'Look!' exclaimed Karin, part rising to grasp the back of my seat. 'Look at that! It's our cryovolcano!'

'Oh, this is wonderful!' declared Sunita, pressing hands to her cheeks.

'So tell me, what exactly causes it?' I asked as we hovered some distance away from what at once struck me also as a most awesome, a most fascinating spectacle.

'Where Titan's crust has ruptured,' Sunita explained, 'liquid water and ammonia from the ocean deep below erupts through frozen methane and water ice then itself freezes instantly into ice flakes.'

'Well what an amazing sight it is,' Karin said with an enthusiasm until now much less in evidence.

'Quite amazing, yes,' agreed Sunita, 'but unfortunately it is samples of erupting fresh from this we need to collect if you, Brett, think it is possible without taking risks.'

'Sure, we can do that,' I said, attempting to convey a reassurance I didn't altogether feel. I took full control of the skimmer. This was not going to be easy and programming her to do it was not an option because she would not attempt anything even moderately risky with people onboard. We had to remain upwind of the volcano because on the other side we'd be hammered by fragments as they were blasted away from it. Anything further down and laying on the ground would, I guessed from Sunita's comments, be contaminated. The best place to approach had to be near to the top of the column where the stuff was slowing, falling and about to be carried away from us by the wind. I also didn't want too much of it hitting our rotor blades. We were very near now and Orion cut in with a warning, 'Brett, you should proceed no closer.'

'It's okay!' I responded and she took the hint; this being a result of the personality profiling she would have done on me as well as the others. She knew I'd be taking little notice but still would act if real danger threatened. Just what she might do I had really no time to think about. We could hear the rising torrent before us roar and crackle. We could see rolling clouds of methane and who knew what else swept away from within the column to vanish in a hazed distance. The skimmer also considered we were entering into a perilous situation and I was obliged to cancel her flashing lights and verbal warnings. She was nagging the way she was supposed to but I needed to concentrate. I edged us forward and up, as close as I dared to the top of this crazy, skywards gushing monster. Even so, bits of ice like oversized, flattened hailstones clattered alarmingly hard and loud against our protective canopy and kettledrum rattled against the fuselage to our rear. We rocked back and forth as I tilted the skimmer aside, enabling our scoops to reach out and grab as much as was needed. None too soon did I back the skimmer away as right then the fountain surged momentarily higher. We were well clear and I wondered once again how Karin might be feeling.

'Wonderful!' exclaimed Sunita as we hovered to watch the spectacle before us. 'Brett, you did it!'

'All in a day's work,' I shrugged.

'And we're still alive!' declared Karin, reaching from behind to grasp my shoulder. 'Well done!'

We remained for several minutes before this, a kind of living entity spawned from the depths of Titan and risen to express itself in terrible grandeur. Then it was time to go. I swung about to head up above the volcano and out of the valley with wind-driven ice flakes racing for a time beneath us, then I had the skimmer take over once more. As my two passengers remained quiet for a while I sat back and I thought for some moments what it might be like to stand alone in that valley, if stand there anyone ever could, and to watch something that pulsed with sound and light; a compelling vision in a realm of grim desolation. I imagined myself looking on with a mixture of fear and reverence, mesmerised by a kind of life force within it that reached into my mind with the words, 'Stay here. Stay. Stay and gaze upon me forever.'

On leaving the valley our final task was to locate that old probe and see if possible what had happened to it, although this had never been high on our list of priorities and was something now of an anticlimax. Meanwhile, far to the horizon, we observed another of the TSS shuttles, this time ascending and no doubt charged with liquid methane. In the many hours we'd been down at the surface, there would have been time for both shuttles to make sufficient journeys to fill the waiting tanker. Our not spotting more of their activity was due to their being at times below Titan's horizon. We flew some seventy kilometres north-east over the ice-mountains to a dune field crossed by a bubbling methane river then slowed at a few metres above a flattish area. Our lights flooded the ground below and I said, 'We're over the specified location but our sensors don't register anything.'

'Ah,' said Karin, sounding perfectly calm, 'then this part of the crust may have moved as it had with the Huygens lander.'

I took the skimmer up higher then, 'Got it,' I said. 'You're right, it's shifted east by a few metres. I'll take us right over it.' Our lights picked out only what looked like the coarse brown sand we'd seen elsewhere but our sensors did reveal the probe. 'It's over a metre below the surface and tilted at an angle,' I informed them as the concealed image appeared on our display. 'It may be intact but the skimmer can't dig down that far and even if it could the thing will be too heavy to lift out with all that frozen stuff piled on top of it. I'll grab a chunk of whatever it is directly beneath us then maybe that will give us a clue later as to how the probe ended up buried down there.'

I was about to do just that when Orion's voice came loud and clear through the skimmer's own system. 'Brett, the cargo vessel is leaving Titan orbit and is turning sunward.'

'Is there nothing you can do to stop her?' I asked.

'No, not now we have allowed her to move out of my force field. Shall I continue to keep you informed?'

'No need,' I answered since we already knew what was going on. 'I'll deal with Viktor in good time.'

'Then we're through down here aren't we,' said Karin.

'We are through here,' I replied and I suspected her misgivings were far from laid to rest. I called on Orion to lower her orbit and we ascended through blustering mists to rejoin her where the skimmer bay was open and ready for us to enter. Once Orion was re-established in higher orbit with the space station we waited as the bots did their preordained job of delivering the containers we'd brought up with us between there and our mother ship. After the sterilisation procedure of these and storage of our environmental suits we stepped out of the bay to find Arnold waiting to greet us. I was relieved to see no sign of Viktor because right then I was angry and needed more time to consider my admittedly limited actions, the worst of which would be to confine him to his quarters should I consider him a danger to our operations. The four of us agreed we'd talk more over dinner. Arnold headed to his quarters, where, to alleviate his curiosity over a place he might never care to see first hand, he'd go through and lose himself in some of the recordings we'd sent back. Sunita would keep herself occupied with the new samples in Orion's laboratory so Karin and I retired to our own private space.

When we were alone I said to her, 'You put a good face on it but you were still not happy to be down there, I know it.'

She looked at me, kissed me, then answered, 'Brett, I never thought I would utter such words but Titan has affected me. I feel as if something malignant was reaching out to touch me – to touch us all.'

I understood what she was saying and I told her so but while I didn't see things that way I had no wish to make her feel any more uncomfortable over it. Yes, Titan was pretty forbidding though Sunita appeared unaffected by it during her one visit. I guess she was far too occupied by the chemistry of the place to have it get at her. Karin would have her own report and assessments to compile but I doubted she'd make her misgivings known there. We rested a while, picked up news from Earth and Mars then as soon as the allocated time to eat was signalled we made our way to the dining area. Arnold and Sunita were already present but Viktor's seat remained empty.

Gesturing to the vacant chair I asked Arnold, 'Have you seen anything of our friend, lately?'

'Not for some time, no. I wanted to go over to the station with him for a look-around while you were down on the surface but the guy refused outright and said it was because there was no gravity over there. That I could understand because I'd honestly forgotten about it being so while you were away. He turned rather unpleasant when I asked him if I could take a look once you were back as he intended to return there himself.'

'Did he now - and you haven't seen him since.'

'No but could be he's still over there.'

'Well let him stay wherever he is,' I responded. We were used to Viktor not being around much of the time and I think on this occasion it suited us more than it had any time earlier. 'And what's the situation with those samples?' I asked Sunita.

'They are in our laboratory and stored at Titan surface temperature,' she answered. 'I will continue with a full analysis tomorrow. We still have a day or two in orbit here do we not should another visit to the surface be needed.'

'We do but I figured on one more day only, our fourth, unless a fifth is really necessary. Don't forget, it's going to take us longer getting back as Earth and Mars themselves will have moved further away.'

'Could be that's why Viktor was in such a hurry,' said Karin.

'Could be,' I agreed. 'We'll see what he has to say tomorrow if he's around by then.'

We sat a while in the dining room to watch broadcast news mainly from Earth, Arnold's main interest being the election of the next UAS president. How casual this whole project of ours had become compared with those not so far off days when every item of planning had to be meticulous. How easy it was now to worry about one extra day when considering the incredibly short time it had taken us to reach Titan.

Chapter 4
Dark Revelations

There were four of us at breakfast on that fourth notional day. We'd just finished viewing a 'hope to see you back here soon' message from Joe and others from the IC when Sunita prompted me to ask about our missing crewmember. She was understandably curious to know what he'd been doing with his allocated samples. I touched my earlobe to ask, 'Orion, has Viktor Saroyan returned from the orbiter? Inform us openly, please.'

'No,' came her reply, 'his presence has not registered with me since after I returned from taking you down to lower orbit on your second descent. He has not returned from the space station.'

'Then,' I asked, 'can you confirm if he's actually in there?' though I'd guessed the answer already.

'I have no communications access to the interior of that facility beyond the flexible airlock.'

'Oh,' said Karin, 'then he must have been without gravity also during the time Orion was detached from the station to bring us back.'

'Maybe he had an accident because of it,' said Arnold with more than a hint of humour. 'You know, floated up suddenly and whacked his head on the ceiling.'

'Might have knocked some sense into him if he did,' I muttered.

106

'Now–now,' grinned Karin, 'he probably thinks he's doing the job he's supposed to do.'

'And I'm doing the job I'm supposed to do,' I responded. 'Orion,' I asked, 'are you able to contact Viktor Saroyan through either of his personal communicators? Just check to see if they're active.' Now that should have been easy enough since Viktor had the earlobe kind we all used as well as that implanted device he'd been so cagey about. We waited. Expectant seconds passed before Orion answered, 'I have no response from either but it is possible he may have shielded himself.'

'Shielded himself,' I muttered. Well that did sound like Viktor, but why would he need to do that at present? We finished eating and went about our businesses, in my case the gymnasium followed by a shower, coffee and a long discussion with Arnold about the future of spaceflight. The evolving technology of the hyperdrive was his pet subject, naturally. I'd been back in our quarters a while with Karin and lunchtime was approaching when my earlobe pinged. It was Sunita. 'Brett, will you come to the lab right now, please!'

I turned to Karin, saying, 'Sunita wants me at the lab – it sounds urgent.'

'Shall I come with you?' she asked.

'Maybe you should,' I answered, so we left our quarters and hurried along the ship to where an anxious Sunita was waiting with the lab security door held open. 'Sounds like you have a problem,' I said as she moved back to let us through.

'Brett, Karin,' she breathed, 'you had better look at this.'

We stepped over to a group of three illuminated cabinets set against a wall, each sealed and faced with an armaplast screen and all three equipped inside with manipulating devices, probes, read-outs and other remote control test facilities. Before each unit was a console with controls and glowing indicators. The internal temperature of the first cabinet showed minus one hundred and eighty degrees Celsius and Titan surface pressure with an atmosphere of mainly nitrogen. We gathered before this and Sunita explained, 'The flask you see in there contains material collected from the river estuary on your first visit. That river, I checked, is part fed from a cryovolcano smaller than the one we visited and carries frozen water crystals originating as liquid from Titan's subsurface ocean. The liquid methane contains also most of the organic complexes necessary for life as we know it.'

'We always suspected there was life in that ocean.' Karin said, 'but never managed to reach it.'

'Wait, please!' she snapped. Karin glanced at me, puzzled, as we shifted to the second cabinet. 'In that container is a small quantity of material lodged within the lander you recovered. It is still kept at minus one-eighty.' She looked hard at us both before announcing, 'Within this I identified DNA.'

'What!' Karin exclaimed. 'But they took a great deal of care even in those days to ensure nothing was contaminated.'

'It seems here they may not have succeeded,' Sunita responded.

'What kind of DNA is this?' I asked. 'Human?'

'No,' she replied, 'it is not human, it is fungal DNA. I have yet to determine to which group it belongs. There are almost two hundred thousand species known on Earth.

'Are you really saying the Huygens lander carried fungal spores?' Karin asked.

'Karin, Brett, at present I can think of no other explanation for I find no evidence of genetic material in the other samples though they are of course from limited areas and none has ever been reported in samples returned to Earth by probes. But there is more you have to see.'

In perplexed silence we moved to the third cabinet and stared through the armaplast screen. Behind this, contained within a flat, transparent tray, was what looked like a viscous, irregular form. It was dull orange, some twenty centimetres at its widest and a few millimetres thick. As we peered closer Karin exclaimed, 'Oh - it's moving!'

Slowly, within the container, parts of the thing advanced and retreated as if it was searching or feeling its way around. 'Sunita,' I demanded, 'what the *hell* is that?'

'I will go briefly over what is already known and what I have learned,' she answered. 'What you see here was another sample of material removed from the lander you recovered. Primitive forms of life may, no *do* I'm sure exist in the relatively warm, sub-surface ocean but when this water emerges from cryovolcanoes above the ruptures in Titan's crust, it freezes, as we already have witnessed. Those life forms I speak of undergo molecular reconfiguration. They adjust to the surface temperature and therefore may no longer be identified as living material. It is only a guess but through the conditions we find on Titan this may be a form of self-preservation. Some plant viruses on Earth can readjust when outside their host and likewise are no longer regarded as being alive.

'What you have here is life on the edge isn't it,' said Karin. 'It's life just waiting for the right circumstances to make it happen and adding genes has created something quite different - something new.'

'That is so. Water must at some time have oozed up or been diverted through the site where the lander rested those many years. What we have here would be dormant except that I have raised the temperature inside the cabinet to fifteen degrees Celsius. The fungal DNA has successfully integrated with certain water-borne complexes originating from beneath the crust and we have before us a truly living substance consisting of massed eukaryotic cells; that is cells containing genes within a nucleus.'

'It seems,' said Karin, 'that with some of Titan's complex organic chemistry, you might synthesise a number of different life forms if you add a few viable genes and these will become active when the temperature is high enough.'

'It would appear so,' breathed Sunita as we continued to stare. 'We have here two potential life ingredients combined to act now as one viable organism. A kind of symbiosis if you like – except that what we have here you will not like at all.'

'So what are you saying?' I asked. 'Is it dangerous? What would happen if this stuff got into a biodome on Mars or someone's garden on Earth?'

Sunita looked from me, to the enclosed specimen, then back again. 'Before calling you in I ran a thorough analysis on this sample. I added a small percentage of oxygen to simulate Earth atmosphere so as to see what might happen. In some ways this behaves like a slime mould. Each individual cell is no more than that but when en-mass as we see it here, it exhibits a group ability to search for a way out of its present confinement. I have tested it with a solid nutrient and -.'

'You mean you fed the thing!' I interrupted.

'Yes, Brett, food *is* what I mean. I find, however, it does not engulf this but invades with hyphae which dissolve the food from within by means of enzymes, then absorb and digest the resulting nutrients. By this means it behaves also as a fungus.'

'So what'll it eat?' I asked.

She hesitated then replied, 'I believe from my tests it will invade and consume almost anything organic - living or dead.'

'It sounds rather dangerous,' Karin remarked in a low voice.

'It would be extremely dangerous if released into an oxygen rich environment,' said Sunita. 'And Brett asked me a moment ago what would happen if it entered the human environment; well I will tell you, I believe it would develop fruiting bodies which means it would spread rapidly by spores.' She looked hard at both of us then added, 'It could be, no, it would be catastrophic! I will now disable this – this, whatever we wish to call it by dropping the temperature back to minus one-eighty and extracting oxygen from the enclosure.'

'Now wait!' I exclaimed. 'The Huygens lander might still have traces of this stuff lodged inside. We had no reason and no chance to clean all of it out before it went into the spare bay of the space tanker and that's now heading back to Mars then on to Earth. What's in there could already be infected! And Viktor Saroyan will have some of it in his lab onboard the space station.'

'I can't imagine he'll have done much with it,' said Karin, 'he wouldn't have that kind of knowledge – or would he. I think we should get hold of the stuff and incinerate it whether he likes it or not.'

'Sure, whether he likes it or not,' I agreed, then I added, 'He must still be there so better if I make my way over right now and deal with it.'

'I must come with you,' insisted Sunita. 'The cabinets in his laboratory will do the same job as those we have here except they are designed for use where there is no gravity. The temperature inside them can probably be raised high enough to kill the samples he has so that is what we must do. It is important also that I look at what he has been attempting in there.'

'I'd be interested to know that as well,' added Karin.

We made our way to the control deck where we encountered Arnold who commented upon our purposeful progress. 'We're headed over to the TSS laboratory,' I informed him. 'There's something pretty serious going on, maybe dangerous, but if you still want to take a look in there now is your chance – but if Viktor's at home don't expect a warm welcome.' As soon as he'd answered, 'Sure thing,' I called Orion to ask, 'Has Viktor Saroyan returned yet from the Titan space station?' Had he done so, had he been asleep in his quarters, I'd have demanded he accompany us to answer any questions Sunita might have.

'Viktor Saroyan has not returned,' came the reply.

'Then is the flexible airlock to the space station pressurised and ready for use?'

'It is pressurised and ready for use,' Orion assured us.

We were on our way past the bay housing our skimmers when I said, 'Hold! I think we should put on e-suits before we go over there. Let's do that.'

'Is it really necessary?' queried Arnold.

'Dunno,' I shrugged, 'it's just a feeling I have, but I reckon we ought to – okay?'

'I agree,' said Karin.

'And I most certainly do,' added Sunita. 'We must take great care until we find out what has been happening.'

'Very well,' nodded Arnold, 'I'll go along with that.'

We suited up then continued along to the dorsal airlock. With this sealed behind us I went ahead, followed by Sunita, Karin and Arnold, up the awkward, flexible passage. From there we entered the space station airlock where, hoping Viktor hadn't altered it, I keyed in the standard entry code. He hadn't. We waited until the inner door opened fully, expecting to be faced by an indignant Viktor, but the amply lit corridor before us was deserted. As we moved inside I recalled from an earlier virtual exploration that to our left lay the storage and accommodation areas and to our right the research and laboratory section. We stood a while, still in anticipation of Viktor making an appearance, a confrontation maybe, but I insisted we did not remove our helmets even though the indicators on the wall before us showed environmental conditions as optimal. Wearing our suits and keeping our helmets on may not have seemed altogether necessary at the time but it was probably the most important decision I made in my entire life.

'Let's go find him,' I said. 'Maybe he's asleep.' With that in mind we made our way to the accommodation area, passing by the molecular recycling unit and the food and equipment storage where everything was secured in racks to deal with what normally would have been a non-gravity situation. Opposite this was the power core then the small gymnasium with muscle-exercising equipment and further along, the crew quarters. The accommodation section was in near darkness but the main lights went on as we entered. Nobody spoke as we stood to look around. There were a number of personal items scattered about the floor and when Orion was decoupled these would have floated freely about the room. This, I assumed, was the reason, because among them was a single discarded shoe. Strange as this must have appeared to all of us, no one made comment except for Arnold who muttered, 'Untidy isn't he.' There were six individual rooms designed to enable sleep in weightless conditions but we looked about to find five of these open and obviously unused. The sixth, however, did show signs of occupation. The reading light was on next to a recently used and much dishevelled bed. More personal possessions were visible there also as well as on the floor close to it. 'He's obviously not asleep and dreaming,' I said.

'Then where the hell is he?' muttered Arnold. 'Looks as if he left in a hurry.'

'If Viktor was up and awake,' said Karin, 'he'd surely realise by now we were on board.'

'You'd think so wouldn't you,' I said, 'Well as he isn't on board Orion and he isn't around here, there's only one other place he can be unless he's stepped out into space.'

'If you mean his precious laboratory,' said Arnold, 'he isn't going to appreciate our pushing our way in there, is he.'

'I don't give a damn whether he does or not,' I countered, 'we still take a look in there.'

We retraced our steps past the main airlock and took a left turn, and there we stopped abruptly. Laying on the floor as if cast hurriedly aside was the other shoe and the upper half of a crew suit that could only be Viktor's. We stepped around both and hesitated at the laboratory door.

'There's something very wrong here, isn't there,' said Karin.

'I feel it, too,' said Sunita.

'There definitely *is* something wrong,' I breathed.

We stood listening a while but still there was only silence. I reached out and, finding it unlocked, slid the outer door open. For safety reasons the lab had its own airlock but there was room in this for only two people at a time. Arnold pushed inside with me, keeping the outer door open while Karin and Sunita followed close behind. I was surprised to find the laboratory in darkness except for the glow of consoles but as Arnold and I entered with the other two about to join us, the automatic main lights came on. I'm sure none of us knew what to expect but the scene in that laboratory defied for some moments my understanding of what was and what was not real. Then the starkly illuminated horror that confronted us became clear. Amid broken sample flasks and other scattered items, Viktor lay sprawled face up by a storage unit at one side the room. Clusters of pallid stalks resembling tufts of white grass blades protruded from the softer parts of his body, through where his eyes had been and through his nose, mouth, cheeks and throat. In the area of his lower chest and stomach, the stalks had penetrated his shirt and further down they had burst through and extended also from the lower half of his crew suit. Some of the thicker, longer stalks bore at their tips oblate spherical caps of a deep orange colour. Spread immediately about him appeared clusters of that same viscous material we had observed in the third cabinet of Orion's laboratory, each small but altogether much more in quantity than the original sample. Slowly, almost imperceptibly, some of them began moving toward us.

A groan from Arnold of, 'What is this - what the fuck are we seeing here!' broke a shocked silence.

Karin, her eyes closed, turned away gasping, 'Oh – oh no!' and placed hands against her helmet in an attempt to dismiss the sight we'd come upon.

Sunita, statue-still, continued to stare open-mouthed at this vision of mind numbing insanity.

'We must get out of here now!' was all I could say though I did have presence of mind to ensure the scene was recorded through my helmet camera as the three made a hurried exit. We were out of there and I had the airlock doors closed hard and fast behind us. We stood for tense seconds in the corridor with little idea of what to say or do next.

Turning to Sunita I said quietly, 'Looks like he mishandled that stuff you showed us.'

'It must have been yesterday,' she breathed. 'I'd say that is when it must have been to have spread as far as it has. Perhaps he was in the crew quarters when it began to take hold of him. It must have been affecting his lungs, his brain and making his flesh burn.'

'Maybe he panicked,' I said. 'Maybe he no longer knew what he was doing when he headed for the laboratory.'

'Possibly so,' agreed Sunita. 'He breathed in the spores and now it is feeding on him, consuming him from inside and very quickly in this Earth-like atmosphere. And, Brett, those things on the stalks are fruiting bodies – they will give out millions more spores.'

'Those spores will have spread everywhere,' added Karin. 'They could be all over our suits now.'

Arnold stood gazing down at his opened hands as I said, 'There'll be the usual means of sterilising ourselves before we leave here then we'll do it again when we're back on Orion. That area connected to the main airlock that's used for suit storage - it'll be through there.'

'Let's get in and do it right now!' exclaimed Arnold. 'I feel my flesh crawling already.'

The suit storage and sterilisation facility we entered was similar to that on Orion. The sterilisation unit we took full advantage of before quitting the space station via the flexible airlock. On our return I detached the flexible airlock altogether from Orion before we stepped into our own sterilisation unit. After what we'd witnessed and with some idea as to what it meant, absolutely nothing could be left to chance. We gave ourselves a double dose of chemical and ultra-violet in spite of Orion assuring us the first time around that, 'You are free of all external organic material.' We discarded the e-suits and kept to our crew outfits but no one spoke until we'd made our way to the control deck. Once there I said, 'That methane shipment is way ahead of us. I'll warn Joe to make sure it stays high in Mars orbit and no one goes near the thing until the lander it's carrying and the cargo bay are sterilised at least twice over in space by robots and I'll include the scene we witnessed inside the Titan space station. As far as Earth is concerned I'll relay it to the International Council for their attention only and hope we find out who's responsible for what, but I'll not send to the UAS or to Frontier mining.'

'Why not the UAS or Frontier?' asked Arnold.

'We can have the International Council deal with the UAS on our behalf as they see fit and as for Frontier it's because I don't trust them. Simple as that.'

'Your message will take over an hour and a half to reach Mars,' said Karin.

'Okay but at least Joe will be warned in plenty of time.'

'I will return to our own laboratory,' said Sunita. 'I must see what can be done to effectively destroy this life form under Earth-like conditions.'

'But what can we do about the space station?' asked Arnold. 'The whole place may be dangerous.'

'The whole place *will* be dangerous!' declared Sunita. 'Some of those spores could easily have passed from the laboratory to other areas of the space station via ourselves if they were not there already – as I think they must have been.'

'At least it will never go back to Earth,' I said, though it didn't take me long to reach a more positive conclusion. 'The TSS, all of it, must be destroyed. I'll include my intention to do so in the messages.'

'Won't Frontier Mining object?' asked Arnold. 'It is their property after all. And how d'you propose to do that – let it burn up in Titan's atmosphere, or what?'

We had the means of achieving what I'd proposed right then, through Orion's newly installed weapons system; blowing the space station apart, that is. Then Arnold, as with just about everyone else on Mars and on Earth, would be made aware of Orion possessing such deadly means when I wanted to retain secrecy there for as long as possible. No, blowing the TSS apart wouldn't do. In any case, spores could descend into Titan's atmosphere. To Arnold's first question I replied, 'I don't give a damn whether Frontier objects or not.' To the second I gave a few moments thought before answering, 'Not in Titan's atmosphere - no. She might not burn up completely and some of those spores could escape and end up anywhere around the surface.'

'But in the temperature down there they'd no longer be active,' he countered.

'Maybe not but future visitors, human or robot, could pick the things up and carry them back to Earth or Mars. Let's make sure that can never happen. The space station is still locked into our gravity field; we can take her out of Titan orbit, head her towards Saturn then release her to go on her way where she'll burn up in the planet's atmosphere. End of problem.'

'We *have* to do that, yes!' declared Karin.

'An excellent plan,' agreed Sunita as she turned to leave us, 'then it all will be gone forever.'

I imagined that before long, Viktor's body would be an all but unrecognisable, shrunken mass covered entirely by those horrific stalks; a kind of grotesque white porcupine. I had Orion transfer the images from Viktor's laboratory and add these to the message I dictated. This included our intention to destroy the TSS and all it contained, together with its pair of shuttles. I also asked Orion to work out a time and trajectory for undertaking the task. The answer came back almost at once; it seemed there would be no problem whenever we wished to do it. By then we had a meal break due, Sunita had rejoined us and whether anyone felt like eating or not we sat and tried to relax in the dining area with no more than subdued conversation. That final image of Viktor Saroyan wasn't going away any time soon. Apart from what we'd experienced in the space station we also discussed our overall situation at Titan and agreed we would terminate our stay in orbit there and set off sunward before the beginning of the next work period; that would be equivalent to our fifth working day and within our original plans for what that was now worth. At one point Arnold was staring hard at me and said, 'But what if a few of those spores did somehow make it into Orion with us, you know, through the flexible airlock – what then?'

'You trying to cheer us up?' I muttered. But I couldn't blame him for thinking that way and I was already planning on what to do should symptoms of infection occur in any of us. I would programme Orion to intercept the tanker, couple to her if possible then have both head directly into the sun. If she was unable to couple then she was to blast the tanker into shreds then head off on her own to ultimate destruction. But for now, Sunita would return to our laboratory to further study that organism, entity, or whatever anyone cared to call it, that we humans had unwittingly brought into existence on another world.

With the space station still in our force field I instructed Orion to move us into an appropriate position for launching the thing on its way to Saturn. For reasons you already know, we couldn't programme it to use its own manoeuvring engines as Orion was unable to access its system. The impetus would come from Orion before final detachment. Within ten minutes we were on our way, accelerating toward the ringed giant that dominated the sky. None of us had, on this occasion, considered it necessary to sit down as we watched Saturn grow slowly larger on the main display. At some five hundred thousand kilometres from the edge of the planet's ring system, at the time tilted slightly upward from our perspective, Orion released her charge from our gravitational hold. It would take the TSS many hours to get there but that hardly mattered because she and all she contained would be gone forever.

We'd returned to Titan orbit when Arnold asked, 'That old rocket powered tanker – is it to stay where we left it?'

'I see no reason to leave the thing hanging about up there,' I answered. 'We still have control of it so I guess it can follow the space station.' Orion confirmed this could and would be done as soon as we caught up with the tanker which was, you will remember, in a higher and therefore slower orbit than our own above Titan. We soon drew close enough and it was a welcome diversion to our thoughts on seeing her rockets ignite and the abandoned tanker start upon her final journey at a far more leisurely speed than had her immediate predecessor. After her image vanished against the mellow glow of Saturn we spent a short while longer in subdued conversation before the responses to my message came through. I accessed the one from Mars first. There was a joint message from Joe and Amalia expressing their amazement at our news and the shocking images I'd included but they again made it very clear they were hoping to see us home soon. The International Council seemed unsure what to make of the Viktor Saroyan affair but their representative praised us for our work on Titan. There was only a token acknowledgement from the

UAS so from that I concluded the IC had given them basic details but left further communication to ourselves.

Karin and Arnold remained on the control deck while I returned to our quarters where I could sit and think alone. In those few minutes of reflection my thoughts turned once more to the Titan space station, now without our force field and our gravity. As she approached the outer limits of Saturn's atmosphere she would begin to increase speed under the planet's own gravity. She would still have her own internal power. All her systems would be working, her air conditioning and her lights. The consoles in her laboratory would be glowing and there would be Viktor's part-digested body, a limp, grotesque, white-bristled puppet floating about the room, arms reaching out amid a jostling array of broken and loose equipment. On falling deeper into the atmosphere the space station would further accelerate and begin to heat up through friction. She would initiate proceedings to try and cool the interior down and she would issue warnings throughout in tones of increasing emergency. On descending further still her systems would begin to fail, her back-up lights would go on then all would succumb to the remorseless rise in temperature. With roaring intensity she would begin to burn with Viktor's body pirouetting about that hellish laboratory until all was consumed in a purifying, screaming blaze.

Then another thought – the Titan space station would have been all along transmitting its own status data to Frontier. They'd probably know nothing of Viktor's fate but would wonder at his silence and would be aware of their prime property being removed from Titan orbit and its eventual demise by virtue of Saturn. I hoped it would keep them guessing until our return.

Karin and Arnold had waited for me on the control deck and Sunita was still at work in our laboratory when Orion confirmed our final departure from Titan orbit. The main display showed real world vision and already we were turning about with the immense form of Saturn swinging across to momentarily blot out the darkness of space and its spectacle of gleaming stars. Once again we didn't feel it necessary to use the seats.

Orion had already turned sunward and was close to initiating acceleration phase when it happened. 'Red alert!' she declared, 'I must respond now!' On the main display, close to the looming image of Saturn, a small bright dot flickered, its position identified clearly by a flashing red circle. In an instant the dot expanded in a vivid glow and was gone.

'Orion,' I demanded, 'what the hell was that?'

'A hypervelocity projectile,' came the reply. 'I did not have time to move from its path. It had to be vaporised or it would have passed through and possibly destroyed us.'

'Where did it originate?' I asked, thankful our interplanetary home from home had been fitted out with such an effective weapons system. It seemed a high-powered beam pointed in the right direction could work wonders.

'It originated from a mobile satellite at less than one thousand kilometres distance,' came the answer.

'Do you have more details?' I asked. 'Probe the thing if you can.'

'I have done so,' replied Orion, 'It is one of three autonomous weapons systems committed to orbit Titan but unidentified by myself until it was activated. The one closest to ourselves was ordered to attack us. This was a response to our disposal of the space station. It is relaying its present status back to Earth and has reported our probable destruction. The other two satellites are presently behind Titan but one of these will be in a position and able to fire upon us in twenty-four minutes. As I am programmed to protect you I recommend immediate destruction of the hostile satellite before it realises we are unharmed.'

'No, wait!' I exclaimed. 'Let them think it succeeded. You can shield us from any further detection can you not – so activate!'

'This facility is available and is now activated.'

'Fine, then we must continue to receive messages but communicate with no one; not even with Mars unless we really have to. If that message from the satellite that attacked us was picked up by Mars as well as by Earth then everyone will all think we're dead. That, I believe, will be to our advantage though I wish I could inform Joe Van Allen we're okay.'

'It's obvious who's set this up, isn't it,' said Karin. 'Someone's programmed the satellite to attack us. Frontier must be involved and I'd include Viktor Saroyan. They saw us as a threat for more reasons than one.'

'Yes,' I breathed, 'Frontier will have planned those little guardians to operate in defence of their prized possession – presumably to keep away the competition. I recall Joe saying the TSS had put out three satellites of its own but we had no idea at the time what they might be for. I wonder who's running things back on Earth now. Someone high up must be backing Frontier and I have a feeling the tanker will make directly for Earth and not for Mars as originally planned. Orion!' I called, 'The cargo vessel heading away from us on hyperdrive – can you calculate destination from its trajectory?'

'The cargo vessel would appear to be on course for Earth but at this distance I can offer a probability of only seventy percent.'

'That's good enough,' I muttered.

'I think you're right, Brett,' said Karin, 'she's heading for Earth, but surely the authorities there will know what they've done and will act accordingly - won't they?'

'Maybe not; much of this will have been set up prior to hyperdrive when it took years to get here so no one might know officially what's really been going on with regards to Frontier. Like they did once before, I reckon they're trying to run a part of their operations away from Earth without UAS or IC authority.'

Understandably puzzled, Arnold raised a finger for my attention, saying, 'Look, sorry to bring this up right now, but no one said anything to me back on Earth about this vessel being armed. I take it this was done during our stay on Mars. But can you be *that* certain someone is trying to kill us because of our operations at Titan?'

'Orion *was* fitted out during her stay on Mars,' I informed him. 'And you should be grateful after what just happened and would most likely happen again pretty soon had we not acted. And as to why I'm certain – that should be pretty obvious if you recall the events on Mars a few years back.'

'Er, yes,' he responded after a moment's thought, 'I see what you mean, but I still cannot -.'

He was interrupted by Sunita, returning from the lab. 'Brett,' she announced, 'I have run numerous tests on that sample but I find so far it can be destroyed only if the spores and other visible parts are exposed to ultraviolet light. That means at least, any of the material shed from the Huygens lander that was left in orbit will be rendered harmless. Otherwise it is a very complicated organism and able to mutate with ease so that anyone exposed would still die when it infected their brain and internal organs.'

'Very well,' I said, 'but you just missed all the excitement.'

'Excitement?' she queried, glancing open-mouthed at each of us in turn. 'W-what do you -?'

'Someone – something tried to kill us all a few minutes back but never mind. Tell me, is it possible

Viktor could have sent a message to Earth from the space station or from that implanted device of his before it took him over completely?'

'I think - yes, in the earliest stages he could have. He would of course have realised something was wrong but may well have had enough time to do that before his brain was affected.'

'So,' I asked her, 'd'you reckon further research on that nasty stuff you've got in the lab will achieve anything?'

'I can only continue as I am,' she responded. 'There must be some effective means of defeating it altogether, this - this thing for which we have no name. But please understand – if it is ever released on Earth, countermeasures or no, it could not be prevented from spreading.'

'Thank you, Sunita,' I said, 'and I'm sure you'll use Orion's facilities to the full.' I turned to Arnold. 'That tanker is two days ahead of us with Earth now over three days ahead of her and we're pretty certain that's where she's headed. Is she able to match our speed now she's under her own power? What I'm asking is, can we overtake her?'

'She has an earlier version of the hyperdrive so no, she'll not match us, but I cannot give you exact figures as additional work has been done on her since my involvement. If you ask me to guess, I'd say we might just reach her before she arrives at Earth.'

I called up Orion and asked, 'Orion, we need to catch up with the space tanker before she arrives in Earth orbit. Can you do that?'

Seconds passed before the response came. 'At present calculated velocity the cargo vessel will be approaching Earth orbit before we reach close proximity but I am proceeding now.'

'We'll have to catch up with and destroy that space tanker if it looks like Frontier will get hold of her first,' I said as the three of us sat down before the main display to observe the stars beyond. 'They're so desperate to show how efficient they'll be at running the whole show they may not accept the danger involved even if they do try to deal with that other piece of cargo she's carrying.'

'You mean the Huygens lander,' said Karin.

'I mean exactly that. Furthermore, the TSS may be gone but I'd be pretty surprised if Frontier and the powers on Earth associated with them were not planning or even readying a second one equipped with hyperdrive.'

'They indeed are planning another,' said Arnold, 'and I myself was involved with this before leaving Earth.'

'Were you now,' I breathed, then I said, 'Because of Earth's position we have over four days rather than the three plus that it took us to reach Titan. We've somehow to occupy ourselves.' I looked to Karin, adding, 'We can't hang around fretting or feeling agitated so maybe programmed sleep for the first four periods would be the answer. Orion will wake us up beforehand if necessary.'

'I think that will be best,' said Karin. 'I could do with a break from reality.'

'I'll go along with that,' agreed Arnold. 'Some of it I'd rather erase altogether.'

We turned our attention to Sunita who said, 'When I have spent a little more time in the laboratory then I, too, will take an induced but short and deep sleep.' With that she once again left us, as did Arnold who headed for his quarters. On looking at the main display I noticed how Orion was accelerating at a phenomenal rate. But as when leaving Mars, we experienced only that feeling of being gripped by her force field with no other effects. Karin and I went to the dining area, ate and drank a little then retired to our own quarters where we chatted a while before slipping into bed. We lay in darkness for some time, hand in hand, neither of us speaking, but both our minds were occupied by the same subject. Finally, Karin spoke.

'Brett, I watched Virgil Hammond die on Mars and that was gruesome enough but what we saw in that laboratory a while back was just so – so utterly dreadful I think it will give me nightmares for the rest of my life. No, I'm sure it will. And you know because I said it when we were down there; it's as if a part of Titan was laying in wait for us and I keep trying to convince myself we're free of it, that it's really gone away – but has it. A part of it is still here in our own laboratory. I know what I'm saying must sound stupid but there you have it.'

'Karin, we've left Titan behind,' I assured, slipping an arm about her, 'and what we witnessed in that space station lab no longer exists, so what say we programme dreams all of our own rather than choose continual sleep then we'll wake up with better memories.' I appreciated how she felt so programming intermittent dreams might be the right thing to do until that fourth day of our return journey. At least Karin was being honest. So many of us erect a façade, do we not, a façade to hide our true selves, our true feelings and our fears. Maybe I'm like that; sometimes unwilling to open doors and windows to let the light into those dark corners. Karin had expressed herself openly over what we'd seen but I couldn't bring myself to do that, nor it seems could Sunita. I reckon Arnold's response lay somewhere in between. We placed the bedside terminals to our heads, closed our eyes and very gently, very quietly, we whispered our wishes. But she was right in one sense about Titan not having gone away. Some of it was in our lab and a part of it was on its way to Earth.

Chapter 5
A Race Toward the Sun

There was a voice from somewhere beyond. 'Please awaken,' it was saying. 'We are passing sixty-five million kilometres distance to Earth.'

I yawned. I was aching a little. I wondered if I was still dreaming until the message repeated. I turned aside to find Karin gazing at me and she said, 'We have to get ready now, it's our new morning.'

'Yeah,' I mumbled, propping myself up next to her. 'You okay?'

'Yes, Brett, I'm a bit stiff, that's all.'

'Did you manage your chosen dreams?' I asked.

'Oh, I chose three including one that is my favourite. I don't know how many times I've relived it.'

'Let me guess – you were in the park back in Sweden.'

'Yes,' she smiled, 'the park near Stockholm where I used to live and where I played when I was a little girl. You have never shared that with me, have you.'

'No, it seems too personal. I feel it would spoil things for you if I showed up there.'

'That's very thoughtful of you, Brett, but did you go anywhere interesting?'

'I allowed myself only the one; maybe you can guess what it was.'

'That's easy; you'd be alone in your wingship and wandering high above those Martian landscapes you so love.'

'Got it in one, yes. I was alone in the sky at sunrise, flying over the mist-filled canyons and craters, skirting those immense volcanoes as sunlight touched their summits and there I was dreaming within the dream about the meaning of it all.'

'But I wasn't with you, was I. You must let me join you up there in the sky one day.'

'Nobody was with me in the dream,' I said, kissing her, 'nobody ever could be, but what does that matter? What matters more than anything is that you are here when I wake up and always will be, and, yes you'll fly with me once we're home – I promise. But there'll be more time for reminiscing later. Now's the time to get ourselves presentable and head for the control deck before breakfast and assess what's been happening.'

We turned up on the control deck to find Sunita already waiting there. Karin greeted her and I was about to do so when Orion announced, 'I will now begin deceleration to local velocity. Radio transmission time to and from Earth is at present one minute.'

'And what will it be for Mars when we reach Earth?' I asked.

'Transmission time to Mars from Earth will be slightly less than nine minutes.'

'And what's the situation with the tanker?'

'The cargo vessel has decelerated and will enter Earth orbit in fifty-seven minutes. On present trajectory it will assume initial orbit at approximately three hundred and twenty kilometres.'

'Better if we're not shielded any more,' I said. 'I want them all to know we just flew in. Signal my home base and inform Joe van Allen we're soon to enter orbit around Earth.'

Just then Arnold joined us. I informed him we were slowing and soon would enter Earth navigational space.

'So we're not far from home,' he smiled, glancing at our main display where Earth had become visible with the welcoming sun large and bright.

'Well that depends on where you call home but I wouldn't start packing your things just yet.'

'It is the tanker we must reach first as you well know,' added Sunita.

'Of course,' he said, 'I was checking only our present situation in my quarters and I didn't take that into account.'

'We have been detected and are being scanned by Earth and Moon-based sources and satellites,' Orion announced. 'I am being questioned over our presence. Am I to transmit a standard response?'

'Don't respond,' I ordered. 'Don't tell them anything. It won't be long before we get a call directly from Earth then I'll accept and reply to it.' We'd slowed down and were only three thousand kilometres out from Earth when the first message came though. 'Orion, this is Elaine Hermanns calling you from the International Council. Please acknowledge.'

We had her appear on the main forward display as I replied, 'This is Brett Anderson and we've remained screened until now because our part in the Titan project was placed in jeopardy by another party.'

She stared back at me, puzzled. 'I don't understand; we received a message from Titan some days ago and when contact with you was lost we assumed the worst. What has happened?'

I'd intended to give her a brief outline of those said events when an overriding message came through on our emergency channel, 'You have a priority call direct from Washington!'

Elaine Hermanns hesitated. I raised both hands in a gesture of apology and said, 'Okay Orion, allow the new message.' As Elaine Hermanns faded a new image opened. There were three people stood together in an office setting. The one in the centre I knew well enough, it was Carla Brennan, head of the UAS Department of Energy. The two smart-suited men with her she announced as representatives of Frontier Mining. I'd never before seen either of them although the younger of the pair did strike me as oddly familiar.

'We are much relieved to see you safely returned, Commander,' she announced. 'And with no communication from yourselves or from your vessel these past days it was assumed your expedition had met with disaster - so why have you not made your presence known until now?'

I repeated those few words I had offered to the IC then added, 'But before I go any further, why did Viktor Saroyan re-programme the cargo vessel to head straight for Earth? It was agreed with our own President on Mars, Joseph van Allen, under the auspices of the International Council, that she would go to Mars first since there we were all set up to undertake initial processing in a safe environment. This was all along to be a joint exercise and I was appointed to see it through. That I have done in spite of the gross misconduct displayed by the representative of Frontier Mining and the extreme risk to myself and my crew that resulted from it.'

She hesitated, looked aside, questioningly, at the younger of the two men, a pale, sleek-haired individual, then back to me, saying, 'It may be better if you were to discuss this briefly with Gabriel Hammond, the head of Frontier, who is here with me now.'

I tried not to appear or to sound taken aback when I realised why that guy looked familiar. He had to be a son or at least a close relative of Virgil Hammond, the man who had tried to take over the Martian colonies by armed force prior to our independence. The man whose life I had ended.

'There has been a misunderstanding in our arrangements,' he began after some hesitation. 'Because of the present orbital situation it was considered more favourable to have Earth's consignment delivered here first and -.'

'Hold there!' I exclaimed, 'I was not made aware of any such arrangement and I bet neither was Joe van Allen.'

Just then my earlobe pinged and Orion informed me that we were nearly at pre-determined Earth orbit and approaching the tanker. Beyond the virtual window next to me I could see Earth, now close. We were about to pass over the Pacific Ocean and the morning terminator.

Hammond glanced aside at Carla Brennan then said, 'Our representative appears not to have co-operated fully with yourself and failed also to make the situation clear, therefore we -.'

'He seldom did co-operate,' I interrupted, 'and maybe he was told *not* to make it clear.'

Carla Brennan peered at him again and was looking very uneasy as Hammond said, 'I do not understand what you mean by gross misconduct or extreme risk to your crew. I - we spoke to Viktor Saroyan a few days ago and he informed us all had gone exactly as planned and confirmed there were no problems. I need to speak with him now and I would like to know why the space station, valuable Frontier Mining property, was removed from Titan orbit and eventually destroyed.'

It was obvious right then just how secretive Frontier had been with even the International Council but at least the IC had revealed nothing to them of our message from Titan.

'Really,' I said. 'Has no one told you? You can't speak to Viktor Saroyan because he's dead and a part of what killed him could be stored inside the tanker. The space station we'll discuss when I'm ready so for now, stay away from the tanker and its contents and allow me to take full control. What may be inside there you do *not* want because it might kill you all! D'you get that?'

'*You* don't give orders, Commander Anderson,' he declared, 'that cargo vessel is Frontier Mining property and Frontier is fully authorised to deal with it now it is in Earth orbit. Our personnel must carry out inspections of their own and after a fuller explanation from yourself our own scientists will deal with whatever problems are associated with it.'

I'd no idea what kind of scientists he had but I was more than ever determined this guy was not going to have his way and made it as clear as I was able. 'I repeat, the tanker was supposed to reach Mars first. That was agreed all along as part of our joint operation so as officially approved leader of the Titan project I am *still* in command around here whether you think so or not.' During this time the main display indicated others were attempting to contact us – Euro-Fed, the European Federation, and the International Council. Karin could deal with the Europeans while Orion would offer the IC a standard back-with-you-soon message.

Carla Brennan spoke for over a minute to Hammond then decided to have her say in an attempt to resolve the situation. 'I must confess I am not altogether familiar with some of this but I'm assured that other arrangements for the cargo *were* made between Frontier and officials of the UAS. Why not let things continue as they are for the time being as the tanker is already in Earth orbit then discuss the matter further?'

That had me wondering if those officials might be the ones who had colluded with Virgil Hammond four years back when I said, 'I take it by "other arrangements" Frontier included the satellite close to Titan that tried to blow us apart.'

Unsurprisingly, Carla Brennan appeared not to understand my comment and stared at Hammond, awaiting his response. Hammond turned aside to speak with the other man who had moved out of the picture then he looked back to me, 'We know nothing of those satellites you refer to at Titan; they must be the work of a foreign power.'

'Foreign power my ass!' I responded. I wasn't by now feeling too diplomatic. 'You just used the plural, satellites, when I referred only to one, and as for foreign powers you know as well as I do, that kind of behaviour stopped half a century back under IC agreement.'

'Then it is an old system that should have been decommissioned years ago,' he insisted.

'Quit bluffing, Hammond,' I said. 'No one would have reason to do anything like that until now. We picked up its transmission back to Earth at the time. That satellite knew who we were and who it was talking to so get out of that one! Meanwhile the Huygens lander is still in the tanker's spare bay and since it doesn't belong to you I will deal with it as I see fit – okay!'

Carla thought she saw here an opportunity to cool the situation and said, 'Do whatever is necessary with the lander. It was intended for the Europeans and is their property. After that Frontier should be allowed to take over the methane shipment and deal with any problems it may present. For now I can see no alternative other than my consulting the President.'

With that, her and Gabriel Hammond's images vanished.

'They don't understand, do they,' said Karin, now back at my side. 'Even if our dear Carla had seen what happened to Viktor Saroyan she's unable to accept how very dangerous that tanker and its contents could be because Hammond will be trying all along to reassure her otherwise.'

'Too right,' I said, 'Hammond resents the fact that Mars was to be an equal partner because of what happened to his old man, not to mention the profits Frontier is desperate to make – profits they have no intention of sharing with Mars. He's obviously talked the newly appointed energy department around to his way of thinking from the day we left Mars for Titan. That could account for the so-called business conversations Viktor Saroyan was having on the way out. I guess Frontier saw the change of government in the UAS as much to their advantage.'

During my dialogue with Earth, Arnold and Sunita had stood by to take in what was said but it was to Arnold I now turned. 'Arnold, we have to regain control of that tanker's hyperdrive before Hammond's crew get a hold on it. You designed the thing and have access to all your records so how about it?' I touched my earlobe and said, 'Orion, while we have time you and Arnold must figure out how to take control of the cargo vessel. Confirm you will co-operate fully with him.'

'I confirm,' came the reply loud and clear, 'and I am wholly aware of what you wish to have done.'

'I'll get onto this right now,' said Arnold. Then he was hurrying off to his quarters.

The tanker, at some ten metres away, appeared on our main display, filling the whole area. 'Can we get a couple of bots to her bay where the Huygens lander is stored?' I asked Orion. 'We need to get inside. We need to sterilise everything in there before we take the lander out for stowage inside one of our own utility bays, then we sterilise it again. If the tanker bay is sealed then it will have to be forced open – yes?'

'I will deploy two of our bots immediately,' Orion replied, then added, 'A message is arriving from Mars.' Our main display lit up again and there was Joe van Allen, a man looking highly perplexed.

'Brett, what the hell is going on! You've been out of touch since Titan and now you show up close to Earth. That goddamned Titan facility no longer exists and here I was thinking you'd all gone with it.'

'Joe, I can't hang around to talk with you right now so Karin and Sunita will take over.' I turned to both of them, saying, 'There's a few minutes wait each way but inform Joe of everything that's happened while I deal with the tanker.'

Orion moved us around to the side of the tanker where the Huygens lander was stored then deployed a couple of her bots. This move placed the tanker within our force field, though Orion still had no control over her propulsion or navigation systems. As Karin and Sunita delivered their message to Joe, I watched the bots, metallic spiders, drift by under the guidance of Orion then, glinting sunlight, move into position by the tanker. Quite how they did it I couldn't make out but there was a flash of light and the door of the storage bay hinged upward to reveal the lander. One of the bots carried a small sterilisation unit that it applied to the lander door and to the inside of the bay before its cargo was extracted. Through our virtual windows I could also watch what was going on through the bots' own cameras and did so as they manoeuvred the lander across to our own bay. Once secured in there I'd ordered the bots to sterilise the lander again and then to sterilise each other. You may think I was becoming paranoid about safety and it could be you're right. As you may have noticed, complying with regulations wasn't one of my strong points but maybe you never looked at what happened to Viktor Saroyan. And it might take only one of those spores, just one, to enter a living environment undetected and disaster could follow. As for the Huygens lander, I had no intention of releasing that to the Europeans until our main problems were sorted out.

Karin and Sunita were concluding their message to Joe but we'd have to wait almost twenty minutes before he could respond. I'd intended to contact Arnold but the main display flashed on again and there was Carla Brennan once more. 'This situation has to be resolved,' she began. 'I tried to speak with our new President but as he is wholly preoccupied with other matters during the transition period he leaves the decision on the cargo vessel to myself and to Chief Executive Hammond.'

The guy she now referred to as "Chief Executive" was standing next to her as before. In his voice there was ill-disguised contempt as he took his turn to speak. 'Anderson – oh, forgive me, *Commander* Anderson; as the methane consignment is in Earth orbit, and full control of it at this point can only be undertaken by ourselves, it would seem only reasonable for you to relinquish your claim. I suggest you return to Mars and let our respective governments deal with the matter. I see the cargo vessel is presently within your force field so it will be necessary for me to deploy two of our own shuttles. They will be instructed to manoeuvre close by. They will take over to prevent further interference and they will escort the vessel away. I hope I make myself clear.'

'You still don't get it, do you, Hammond. I am complying with a legal agreement certified by the International Council and your own government and *that* stays.'

'Anderson,' he resumed,' the shuttles will be equipped to ensure your compliance and that is the last I'm prepared to say on the matter!'

I noted, before the conversation closed, how Carla Brennan showed surprise at his comments and it appeared there and then that Hammond had overstepped the mark. Nevertheless, he might well have his way and I'd taken what he said as a direct and possibly acute threat to ourselves. I contacted Arnold and asked, 'Any luck?'

'We can move the tanker out of Earth orbit at local speed,' he replied, 'but we still cannot engage hyperdrive. I can feed in a course of our own so we can direct her out of orbit if that is any use. Orion has all these details so far.'

'Okay then let's get her moving.' I looked down at Earth. We were crossing the night side with a myriad city lights breaking the darkness below and I told Orion to watch out for any UAS launches that were headed in our direction. These would be small rocket powered vehicles from Frontier's own launch facilities but easy enough to detect well in advance of their arrival. Karin and Sunita were still occupied in conversation with the IC but I had little time to figure out what to do next. What *could* we do with this vessel full of liquid methane that was possibly infected? We had a degree of control but unless Arnold and Orion could manage full operation of her hyperdrive she wouldn't be going anywhere soon other than a few hundred kilometres further out from Earth. Should Arnold succeed then it was my intention to have her heading straight for the sun where she and her contents would be utterly destroyed. I was half listening to Karin and Sunita and half occupied with thoughts of the tanker when Orion announced, 'Two rocket vehicles have launched from New Mexico and they have locked onto the cargo vessel. Their time to orbit will be fourteen minutes then they will close upon us in a further seventeen.'

There was a short pause then Arnold pinged my ear. 'Brett, we cannot crack the hyperdrive problem without causing damage to the tanker's control systems but those shuttles I hear are on the way *will* be programmed to operate and take her over again and there's nothing we can do to stop that. Also, we can't be shielded while we're connected to her, if that's what you wanted.'

'Thanks, Arnold,' I said, 'that's made up my mind for me.' What complicated the matter further just then was Karin informing me that, 'EuroFed are about to send up a piloted shuttle of their own and insist we transfer the Huygens lander to it when it arrives. They seem rather concerned about the situation we have here.'

'Can't say I blame them,' I muttered, then to Karin I said, 'Tell them to hold back until we give them the okay to avoid any risks to their shuttle or to the Huygens.'

'I'll do that,' she assured me. 'Oh, and Elaine Hermanns has changed her mind. She now assures me that you really are within your rights in keeping control of the tanker.'

'Well thanks,' I said, 'there's a bit of good news at least,' then I called via my personal communicator, 'Orion keep that cargo vessel moving and tell me when those two shuttles approach and when they try to take her over.'

'I will do so,' came her calmly reassuring response. But there were other instructions, primary and secondary actions, I had to give her and, as Earth turned beneath us into daylight, these I quietly delivered. I'd had us disconnected from the tanker and manoeuvred her with Orion positioned some fifty metres behind. We were in a higher orbit but looking out seemed hardly any further from Earth when Orion informed me, 'Brett, the shuttles are five minutes away and are attempting to establish contact with the cargo vessel.' With his comment that, "the shuttles will be equipped to ensure your compliance," Hammond had made it clear that they were armed and might act against us should we attempt to obstruct them. The man was almost as crazy as his predecessor but it was good of him to warn me so I thought. I looked up at our main display to observe the shuttles approach us above the curvature of Earth. As I watched the short burst glow of their manoeuvring jets I asked Orion, 'Can you probe the purpose of those vessels and assess their danger to us?' I needed to see if Hammond was bluffing here as well.

'They are older tactical weapons once intended to defend orbital assets,' came the reply. 'They are equipped with small projectiles and so are potentially dangerous to us.'

That was all I needed. 'Okay Orion,' I said, 'initiate primary action.' Within moments, as Karin and Sunita stood by me, the shuttles, struck by Orion's beams, disintegrated simultaneously in glorious, flaming silence. In my mind I conjured up the sound of a loud explosion. Explosions could never be heard in space but it sounded pretty good there in my mind. Karin and Sunita were still watching when I called, 'Orion, initiate secondary action.' The tanker next appeared on our display and was beginning to move further ahead of us. She was some two hundred metres distant when, as Orion manoeuvred her into position, the beam hit her dead centre at the rear. Arnold had joined us and with the three present I considered an explanation to be in order. 'We'll let her go as she is,' I informed them. 'Now she's warmed up enough this close to the sun, that hole will have her cargo of liquid methane act like a rocket and help propel her away from here.' Escaping methane vapour blurred the tanker's image for a while then dispersed as she moved further from us. 'If or when anyone tries again to take control of her,' I added, 'there'll be nothing left inside to make it worthwhile.'

'Is she still heading for the sun,' asked Karin.

'She is,' I replied, 'well – probably into close orbit if not direct, but it's going to take her years to get there.'

'Can we not destroy her also?' asked Sunita.

'We could, but the bits and pieces would be a space hazard, as parts of Hammond's shuttles will be until someone clears them up. We'll let the tanker continue on as a long term reminder to the likes of Hammond that he can't so easily have things his own way. Maybe one day the people stationed on Mercury will see her going by.' Orion's voice touched my ear. 'Brett, the International Council wishes to speak with you.'

'Go ahead,' I confirmed. Elaine Hermanns appeared large as life on the main display to announce, 'Commander Anderson, all authorities here are aware now of what has been happening and it has caused what I think we might regard as quite a stir. All governments on Earth are demanding we discuss this matter under the auspices of the International Council and that Mars' authorities should take part also. I will therefore be personally contacting President Van Allen. Meanwhile the UAS has confirmed that no further hostilities will be undertaken by Frontier Mining towards yourselves and no further actions taken over the exploitation of Titan resources until the situation is resolved with the agreement of all parties.'

Well that sounded like a step in the right direction but left us with not much to do for a while. Karin, Sunita and Arnold agreed we'd hang around in Earth orbit and have ourselves something to eat. We had much to talk about in the dining area and we'd all forgotten when we were supposed to be resting as Orion had not been told to continue with the work period reminders. It didn't matter right then because there were decisions to be made. Meanwhile, the shuttle allocated to collect the Huygens lander for the Europeans was on its way up and within an hour would acquire orbit with us. Arnold had decided he'd keep the lander company and hitch a ride back to Earth as the shuttle had accommodation for two passengers. Sunita expressed a desire to return with Karin and myself to Mars. She figured she might continue her researches on the Titan samples in one of our outstations where the risk from those spores would be practically zero. I suggested she contact Joe well before the shuttle turned up, which she did with my full backing. After the irritating but inevitable time delays it came as no surprise to me that he agreed at once to take her on. Sunita, with her expertise, would be an asset to our own scientific community as long as she felt at ease with the Martian deserts. It was then up to her to settle matters with those she had been involved with on Earth until now.

When the European shuttle arrived and connected to our airlock we said our farewells to Arnold, who grinned back at us through the helmet of his environmental suit. We watched the Huygens lander, soon to be a prized museum exhibit, transferred by our bots into the shuttle's ready prepared cargo bay. I hoped they might credit us at the exhibition centre with bringing their treasured relic home in one piece.

How long the debate on Earth would take there was no way of knowing but after Karin and I had spoken again with Joe I had Orion set course for Mars. As the journey would take over a day, skirting around the sun and crossing the orbit of Venus, it would give us an opportunity to catch up on our sleep. We were glad of this because Joe had promised us, "one hell of a party," when we arrived back at Novamerica One, my home base.

***

On our return to Mars Joe was true to his word. The party was held in our biodome main restaurant, naturally, and consisted of around sixty people including Karin, Sunita and myself together with the heads of other bases. Amalia had come down from the space station to join us and we had much to talk about. The food and wine, most of it a product of our own processing facilities, we considered equal in quality to pretty well anything Earth could have supplied. Thinking back on our journey I admitted to all who asked, that yes, Orion had cared for us well indeed and I had gained more respect for machines, though that term was hardly adequate in her case. All in all, though, it was good to be home.

Eight days passed before we received any news from Earth over the Titan affair. Joe had of course been involved in spite of those delays in transmission between Mars and the home planet. Karin and I, together with Sunita, were called into Joe's office where we were greeted also by the smiling image of Elaine Hermanns at the headquarters of the International Council. It transpired that the UAS, under her new president, had agreed with the other powers on Earth, officially, that no one should be allowed a monopoly on hydrocarbon supplies from Titan and that all future dealings over this and with Mars had to be undertaken through the IC as it all along should have been. Adding to the good news was their condemnation of Gabriel Hammond and Frontier Mining for their unscrupulous and negligent approach to the project, with Hammond himself facing criminal prosecution.

Karin and I had discussed all we'd been through, all we'd witnessed, and we knew that memories of Titan would haunt us for the rest of our lives. When she asked me, 'Would you ever want to go back there?' I assured her, 'No, I wouldn't.' I had no need to put the same question to her.

As you are aware, Karin and I often shared dreams but something oddly personal would now and again occupy my mind when asleep, something that Karin would have no desire to witness again – the cryovolcano.

Beneath the looming ghost image of Saturn I moved through that deep, grim and frigid valley of despair until before me arose that monstrous, that magnificent white fountain - a gushing, living entity. I saw it as an expression of life amid soulless desolation and it fascinated me beyond reason. I approached. I listened to its roaring voice and I watched it shimmer, rising and falling, scattering its frozen message into the bleak wilderness beyond.

My thanks to Lynda Buxton for her invaluable assistance
in reading through and pointing out the numerous
textural and other deficiencies in my work.

www.jeffreypeterclarke.com

More books by the author

ELECTRA
I, MEDEA
RETURN OF THE HERO
THE SINGING STONES
THE DEVIL IN EDEN
THE MAN WHO SOUGHT ETERNITY
SHADOW OF THE BEAST
HIDDEN WORLDS Volumes 1 and 2

Available from https://fiction4all.com
And other good book stores.

Jeffrey Peter Clarke